THE GUARDIANS *of* GA'HOOLE

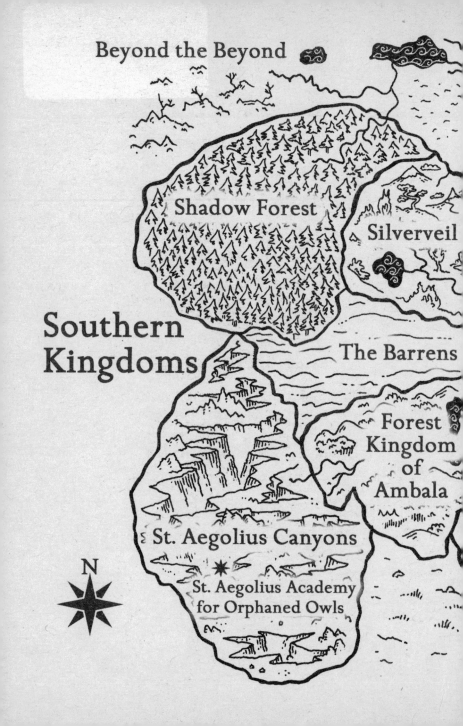

Broken Talon Point

Northern Kingdoms

Peninsula
of the
Spirit Woods

Ice
Narrows

Sea of Hoolemere

Island of Hoole

Cape
Glaux

The Beaks

Desert
of
Kuneer

Forest Kingdom
of Tyto

Soren's Hollow

River Hoole

"You're Hoke, aren't you?
You're the Kielian snake that Ezylryb sent us to find."

GUARDIANS
of GA'HOOLE

BOOK SIX

The Burning

BY KATHRYN LASKY

SCHOLASTIC INC.

New York   Toronto   London   Auckland
Sydney   Mexico City   New Delhi   Hong Kong

No part of this publication may be reproduced in whole or in part, or stored in a retrieval system, or transmitted in any form or by any means, electronic, mechanical, photocopying, recording, or otherwise, without written permission of the publisher. For information regarding permission, write to Scholastic Inc., Attention: Permissions Department, 557 Broadway, New York, NY 10012.

ISBN 978-0-439-40562-1

Text copyright © 2004 by Kathryn Lasky. All rights reserved. Published by Scholastic Inc. SCHOLASTIC and associated logos are trademarks and/or registered trademarks of Scholastic Inc.

Artwork by Richard Cowdrey
Design by Steve Scott

17 16 15   10 11 12 13 14 15/0

Printed in the U.S.A.   40

First printing, November 2004

Northern Kingdoms

N

Glauxian Brothers
Retreat

Hrath'ghar
Mountains

Lagoon
of Moss

Bitter
Sea

Firth
of Fangs

Kiel Bay

Pirates' Lair

Stormfast
Island

Hrath'ghar
Glacier

Bay of
Fangs

The
Tridents

Hock

Everwinter
Sea

Elsemere Island
Glauxian Sisters
Retreat

Ice Talons

Ice
Narrows

Ice Dagger

Dark Fowl Island

Southern
Kingdoms

Contents

Prologue

"Night gathers and your time has come," intoned Barran the large Snowy Owl and monarch of the Great Ga'Hoole Tree. Soren's gizzard tingled with excitement. In some ways it seemed like only last night that he, Gylfie, Twilight, and Digger had traveled through that blinding blizzard and had arrived at the great tree. But in other ways it felt like forever. Now they perched, ready to take the most inviolable oath of their lives: They were to become at last Guardians of Ga'Hoole. As the band of four, along with their close friends and chaw mates, repeated after Barran the oath of the Guardians, their voices blended into one:

"I am a Guardian of Ga'Hoole. From this night on I dedicate my life to the protection of owlkind. I shall not swerve in my duty. I shall support my brother and sister Guardians in times of battle and in times of peace. I am the eyes in the night, the silence within the wind. I am the talons through the fire, the shield that guards the innocent. I shall seek to wear no crown, nor win any glory. And all these things I do swear upon my honor as a Guardian of Ga'Hoole until my days on this earth cease to be. This be my vow. This be my life. By Glaux, I do swear."

CHAPTER ONE

Claws in the Moonlight

I thought you said the prevailing wind was from the south," said Martin, the tiny Northern Saw-whet Owl. "We've been ramming into these northerlies for two days now."

"Don't worry," Twilight said. "It's bound to let up sometime."

"Sometime . . . I do not find that comforting. You're twice my size, Twilight, and with that fat head of yours you can ram through anything."

It was not Martin, however, whom Soren was worried about. He knew that the plucky little owl could handle almost anything. He was in the colliering chaw, after all, and was accustomed to diving into the flaming gales of forest fires. No, it was Dewlap, the disgraced Burrowing Owl, about whom Soren was worried. She had been found guilty of spying for the Pure Ones during the long and perilous siege of the great tree the previous winter. Because she was quite old, and because Boron and Barran, the monarchs of the tree, found "mitigating circumstances" in the fact that she had been misled by the Pure Ones, she was not expelled into the wild. Instead, she would be taken to the retreat of the Glauxian Sisters on Elsemere Island in the Everwinter Sea where she would be left to live out her days.

But that was only one part of the mission. After Elsemere Island, Otulissa and Gylfie were to proceed to the Glauxian Brothers' retreat to learn more about war strategy and find in their library another copy of the fleckasia book that Dewlap had destroyed. Martin and Ruby were to fly to Stormfast Island to search for a Kielian snake called Hoke of Hock.

The most important part of the mission, absolutely vital not only to the Guardians of Ga'Hoole but to every owl kingdom on Earth, was that of Soren, Twilight, Digger, and Eglantine. They were to proceed to the Firth of Fangs in the most northwestern region of the Everwinter Sea to seek out an old warrior named Moss. From Moss, they were to recruit allies for the impending war with the Pure Ones. Finally, they were all to reunite on Dark Fowl Island where the legendary blacksmith Orf crafted the finest battle claws ever known.

But with the wind and their rate of speed, who knew when they would get there? thought Soren. They had been flying for two days already and had not yet reached the Ice Narrows. The mission was complicated and there were time pressures as well. Winter came early to the Northern Kingdoms. It would not be long before the fearsome katabatic winds would set in and ice floes would clog the sea, making water almost indistinguishable from land, and navigation difficult. Soren sighed when he thought of his immense responsibilities and the price of failure. Failure spelled doom in this case. If only they could fly a little faster. But not with Dewlap. It was amazing that the flight therapists back at the tree had gotten the old wreck airborne at all.

Dewlap had been lagging so far behind that Soren had to send Gylfie back to fly with her. Then Twilight, and then Ruby after him. They had all taken their turns, except for Otulissa. Otulissa loathed Dewlap with a deep and abiding passion ever since Strix Struma's death. Otulissa had worshipped Strix Struma, who was distinguished in battle, and was an owl of great learning. She had died in the Battle of the Siege. Soren and the others had tried to reason with Otulissa about it. Owls get killed in battle, they said. Dewlap was nowhere near when it happened. But Otulissa still believed that Strix Struma's death was all Dewlap's fault.

And now, as the leader of this special mission, Soren would have to order Otulissa to fly back to attend Dewlap.

"She'll kill her, Soren," Gylfie said.

"Don't be ridiculous, Gylfie. If word gets back that we didn't safely deliver Dewlap to the sisters, we'll all be in trouble."

"I was speaking figuratively," Gylfie replied. "I didn't literally mean 'kill her.' But that old Burrowing Owl is frail as it is and she's terrified of Otulissa. It might just do her in."

They were flying in a tight triangular formation, which enabled them to punch into the headwind more effectively. Soren peeled off to the other side of the triangle, the side on which Otulissa flew.

"Otulissa, your turn to fly with Dewlap."

Otulissa gave him a withering look. But Soren returned it, his black eyes seeming to get even blacker. "This isn't debatable, Otulissa. I am the leader of this mission. If there is a war —"

"What do you mean *if*?"

"All right, *when* there is a war —"

"An invasion, more precisely." She sniffed.

Soren sighed. Glaux! This Spotted Owl frinked him off. "All right, Otulissa, we all know that you are a strategist for the invasion. At that time you will be the leader and I shall follow your orders. But this is not the invasion. This is a mission to the Northern Kingdoms, and if we don't succeed in reaching our allies, there will be no invasion."

"So what does Dewlap have to do with all this? She is immaterial."

"That she may be, but Elsemere is on our way and it makes perfect sense that we deliver her to the Glauxian Sisters. Would you prefer that she continue to live in the great tree?"

Otulissa blinked. *Soren's right,* she thought. *Do I want that miserable old owl in my feathers forever?* Logic always appealed to Otulissa. She tipped her wing, carved a turn, and headed for the Burrowing Owl at the rear.

Soren breathed a sigh of relief as he saw her fly back. The invasion was something Otulissa had dreamed of for months. She had urged the parliament of Ga'Hoole to finish off the Pure Ones as soon as possible after the siege of Ga'Hoole. But they had waited too long. Only a few months later the Pure Ones themselves launched a surprise attack, not against the Guardians of Ga'Hoole, but against St. Aggie's, where a bad congregation of owls roosted in a stone fortress that was rich in flecks. These strangely powerful magnetic particles could destroy not only an owl's navigational abilities, but, in certain situations, shatter their minds and make them mindless tools for evil.

The owls of St. Aggie's were brutish and rather dumb. They had no idea of the power that possession of the flecks put within their grasp. But the Pure Ones did, and when St. Aggie's fell to them, the parliament of Ga'Hoole began to take Otulissa more seriously. They realized that this counterattack against St. Aggie's was not a matter of vengeance, but a matter of absolute necessity for the survival of owlkind. Flecks in the talons of the wrong owls would make for a disaster of unimaginable proportions. And so it was decided. They must launch an immense invasion of St. Aggie's.

The owls of Ga'Hoole could not do this alone. They would need the help of owls as skilled in battle as they were. The kind of elite fighting force that Ga'Hoole required could only be found in the Kielian League of the Northern Kingdoms, where Ezylryb had come from originally. For more than two centuries these owls, raised in a free society, had fought one of the longest wars in the history of owlkind against the League of the Ice Talons, a brutal regime to the east of the Kielian League. But they had finally won.

Originally, Ezylryb had ordered only six of them go to

the Northern Kingdoms. But Soren had convinced him that this was a complicated mission and had entreated Ezylryb to allow the entire Chaw of Chaws to go. So Martin and Ruby, both superb fliers, joined the mission.

Soren looked down at the battle claws he was now wearing, which had been made by the legendary blacksmith Orf. They sparkled in the light of the moon. Once these claws had belonged to Ezylryb, back in his days as a warrior and commander of the legendary division known as the Glauxspeed. But Ezylryb had given them to Soren. The memory of that moment of the passing of the claws came back now to the young Barn Owl. Once again, Soren could hardly believe it had happened. In his mind, he could still hear Ezylryb's voice: *The claws are for you . . . They are the keys to the Northern Kingdom . . . Every owl will know that you are my ward. You are under my protection as a son might be.*

A son! The thought was incredible to Soren, who had been orphaned so early in life, snatched by the horrid owls of St. Aggie's, and taken to their vile "academy" in the canyonlands. When he had finally escaped, he found that the old hollow where his parents had dwelled for years was empty. He had suspected that his brother, Kludd, now leader of the Pure Ones, had murdered their parents. He had later learned that blood sacrifice of a family member was part of the oath taken when an owl became a Pure One.

Two such different oaths! Soren thought as he recalled the words of the Guardian's oath. He could not even imagine the words of the oath of the Pure Ones.

The wind had begun to shift, making their flight easier. It was now a tailwind, and perhaps, Soren hoped, they would reach the Ice Narrows before dawn. Soren didn't fancy flying in daylight. Even in this wild and frozen country of the north, there might be crows. Only once in his life had crows mobbed him, and he vowed that never again would he fly so recklessly from an old night into a new day. He wondered how Otulissa was faring as Dewlap's escort. Perhaps he should fly back and check.

CHAPTER TWO

Puffling Alert!

Yuoy bis
Tuoy bit
Tuoy bim
Nuoy bimish
Vuoyou bimishi
Vuoyven bimont."

"What are you talking to yourself about, Otulissa?" Soren asked as he slid in next to the Spotted Owl. It was obvious to him that she was not addressing her muttered remarks, which sounded like gibberish, to Dewlap.

"I'm practicing irregular verbs in Krakish," she said. "You know, the language of the Northern Kingdoms. Of course, the Kielian League has a number of dialects, but Ezylryb said all the owls understand basic Krakish."

"Oh. Well, I was just coming back to check on how you're doing."

"As well as can be expected." She sniffed and shot a poisonous look toward Dewlap, who seemed to be completely unaware of her disdain.

"Well, with this wind shift we should be approaching the Ice Narrows just at dawn. I'm going to get a navigation check from Gylfie," Soren said, just before winging away from Otulissa's flank.

"Gylfie, what's our heading?" he asked, flying in next to his best friend.

"North by northeast, but with this wind shift, we're being set a bit to the west. You see." Gylfie flipped her head straight up as only an owl can. "We're two points off the tail of the Little Raccoon. A little complicated because we're so far north the constellations rise in different positions in the sky."

It *was* complicated, Soren thought, and he was eternally grateful that Gylfie was such an excellent navigator. She had been trained in the navigation chaw under the direction of Strix Struma, and Gylfie had been one of her finest students ever. *Glaux forbid that flecks ever messed with Gylfie's brain!* "So you think dawn or before for arriving at the Ice Narrows?" Soren asked.

"More like a little after," Gylfie replied. She glanced at Soren. She knew that flying in daylight worried him. "Look, Soren, I can't imagine that there are any crows around here."

"Let's hope not," he replied.

What they could not have imagined were recklessly flying puffins or, more precisely, pufflings.

Fog had thickened the night into swirls of gray, obscuring the stars and the light of the moon, and it was still at least two hours until dawn. They had been making good headway. The wind was firmly behind them, increasing their speed by two to three knots, when, suddenly out of the woolly air, burst a hurtling bundle of white. Then a squawk split the fog. "Puffling alert!"

"Oh, so sorry, so sorry! Did he miss you?" an adult puffin asked Digger.

"Barely," huffed Digger. Then, "Good grief, *Dumpy?*"

"Dumpy!" Soren, Gylfie, and Twilight gasped in amazement.

"Dumpy?" Martin turned to Ruby. "What kind of name is that?"

"Mine! Mine!" the puffin answered. "And this is Little Dumpy, my son. We thought we'd never see you again, Soren."

"Little Dumpy? Son? You're a father." Soren spoke in a stunned voice. The larger puffin was now flying with the young one tucked firmly under his wing.

"Yes, yes. Isn't it wonderful?"

"Wonderful? But you're younger than we are," Soren

said as he recalled how the band of four had accidentally been blown into the Ice Narrows so many seasons ago. They had been searching for Ga'Hoole but a williwaw had swept them north and they had slammed into the eastern wall of the Narrows, where they had encountered a most peculiar bird family, the puffins. "I can't believe you're a father."

"Well, I am. That's the way it goes with us puffins. We mature early."

Soren and Gylfie exchanged glances. Both had the same thought: *Mature and smart are two different things. Puffins are the dumbest birds ever — even when full-grown. And now a parent! Ridiculous.*

"Are we close to the Ice Narrows?" Gylfie asked.

"I don't know, you're the one with the brains." Dumpy gurgled madly. Gurgling was the puffin form of laughter.

"What are you doing out here, and how come your chick nearly slammed into me?" Digger asked.

"Oh, you've come at a wonderful time," Dumpy replied.

"And what time is that?" Soren asked.

"Puffinflockin-in the nocken."

"Puffa whata?" Twilight asked and then snarled, "Hey, beat it!" as another small puffin crashed into his left wing.

"Puffinflockin-in the nocken is the night the pufflings take their first flight out over the ocean. But they often smash into things or crash-land."

"Yes, so we see," Soren said and made a mental note: *Puffins are such awkward fliers themselves they should not be teaching any bird how to fly.*

"The Ice Narrows!" Gylfie cried out. "Straight ahead."

"Oh, I'm glad someone knows where we're going!" Dumpy cried out cheerfully. "Come along, my Little Dumpette. Follow Papa, and Papa will follow these very smart birds."

A few minutes later, they were crammed into one of the many ice nests that pocked the sheer frozen walls of the Narrows. Puffins nested in the cracks and rocky holes that they were so good at finding in the ice-sheathed walls of the Narrows.

They are also very good at fishing, Martin noticed. "Will you look at that!" he said as he perched on the edge of the nest and looked straight down at Dumpy's mate. She had just come up with a mouthful of fish and was proudly lining them up in a row on the floor of the nest.

"Oh, Tuppa! Lovely, my dear, just lovely," Dumpy said. "Such a mate I have!" He gazed at her with love in his eyes, and then at the fish with equal adoration.

"Now, Dumpy dearest, how did our Little Dumpy do on Puffinflockin-in the nocken? Many crashes?"

"Oh, yes, many. So many!"

"Oh, good!" Tuppa lofted herself lightly from the floor

of the ice hollow and waggled her bright orange feet glee-fully.

"Pardon me, madam." Digger stepped forward. "But I am curious. Why is it good if your child crashes a lot when learning to fly?"

Tuppa froze on the spot. Then her beak began to clack loudly and a tear leaked from her eye. "Now, now, dear!" Dumpy came over and patted her.

"What did I say?" Digger asked. "I didn't mean to hurt her feelings." By this time, Tuppa had thrown herself onto the floor of the ice nest. Her immense chest was heaving with sobs.

"It's nothing," Dumpy said.

"Nothing!" Tuppa squawked and in a flash was back on her feet delivering a swat to her mate. "You call it nothing? Our only child leaves home and you call it nothing?"

"Leaves?" Digger asked.

"Yes. When a young puffin learns how to fly, it flies away. That's it. Gone!" Tuppa began to sob again.

"I can't wait," Little Dumpy said. "I'm not scared at all, and I keep telling Ma that I'll be back. I'll come back and visit all the time."

"That's what they all say!" Tuppa sputtered. "But they don't, do they? Do they, Dumpy?"

"Nope. Too dumb to find our way back to the birth nest," Dumpy senior replied.

It appeared to Soren that Tuppa was still trying hard to blink back tears when her eyes suddenly flew open in alarm. She was peering into a corner of the ice nest. "What is that thing over there . . . that . . . that pile of dirty feathers?"

"Oh, dear," Gylfie muttered.

"Let me explain." Soren stepped forward. "That is an elderly Burrowing Owl. She is not at all well, and we are charged with delivering her to the Glauxian Sisters on Elsemere Island."

Tuppa took a step closer to Dewlap and peered at her. She walked around her as if to examine her from every angle. Suddenly, she plopped down next to the pile of dirty feathers. "Bring me that smallish fish, Little Dumpy."

"What do you mean 'smallish'? Is that what you call a small fish? Smallish, and a big one 'biggish'?" Little Dumpy asked.

"Just bring it, for crying out loud!" Tuppa squawked.

"All right, all right. Don't get your feathers in a twist, Ma." Then under his breath he muttered, "I can't wait to get out of here."

Little Dumpy brought a fish to his mother, and Tuppa

began to feed it to Dewlap, all the while making cooing noises and giving the old Burrowing Owl gentle instructions on how to eat it. "Yes, you little sweetie. Headfirst, that's how we do it. Yes, eyeballs and all — that's the tastiest part. Can't miss those eyeballs. Yummy in the tummy." Tuppa looked up at her mate. "Can I keep her, dear?"

"She's not a baby, Tuppa," said Dumpy.

"In the name of ice, she's not even a puffin, Ma. Even I can tell that!" shrieked Little Dumpy.

"But look how sweet she is, and eating the eyeballs, too," Tuppa said.

"I ate every eyeball you ever fed me," Little Dumpy whined as he looked on enviously at the attention his mother was lavishing on Dewlap.

"Can I keep her?" Tuppa said again.

"I'm being replaced by a raggedy old owl?" Little Dumpy wailed. "Well, that does it!" Before anyone could stop him, Little Dumpy was on the edge of the ice hollow and had launched himself into the wind.

"He's flying!" Big Dumpy shouted. "Look at him go! Nothing like being insulted to get one out of the nest."

"Yes, it works every time. Doesn't it, dear?" Tuppa said.

All of the owls were thoroughly confused. "But I thought you said you wanted him to stay," Soren said. "You were sobbing just a minute ago."

"What's a minute?" Tuppa asked.

"A very brief amount of time!" Gylfie almost roared. "And a minute ago you were sobbing."

"I know. Fickle, aren't I? But I really would like to keep this owl."

"If only," Otulissa muttered.

"No, no, no." Soren stepped forward. "It's not possible. We have our orders, and we must deliver her to the Glauxian Sisters."

"I see," Tuppa said. "Well, I guess I'll just have to lay another egg next season. I wonder if I could hatch an old puffin. You know — no back talk."

"But the chicks are such fun," Dumpy said.

"Yes," Soren said. "I'm sure you will find a baby puffin much more to your taste than an elderly Burrowing Owl."

"To my taste!" Tuppa exclaimed in alarm. "I'm not going to eat the baby, nor the Burrowing Owl. How savage!"

"Oh, no, ma'am. I meant no such thing," Soren replied. "It's just an expression."

"Expression? What's an expression?" Tuppa asked.

"I think it's a kind of fish, mostly found in Southern Waters," Dumpy said.

Oh, good grief. Here we go again, thought Soren.

CHAPTER THREE
The Ice Dagger

I'm exhausted!" Gylfie said as they flew up the Ice Narrows. "Completely and utterly exhausted."

"How can you be exhausted?" Soren asked. "We have a tailwind, and we've been flying for all of five minutes."

"What's a minute?" Gylfie said in a mocking voice. "What's an expression? What's a this? What's a that? That is what is exhausting, Soren. I couldn't take another second, let alone a minute of their stupidity. How in the name of Glaux have they survived as a species this long?"

"Well, there are different kinds of intelligence," Soren replied.

"Don't you mean that there are different kinds of stupidity?"

"Not exactly. We'd be stupid up here. Stupider than the puffins. It takes a special kind of intelligence to live in the north. What do we know about fishing or finding hollows in walls of ice?"

"Hmmm," Gylfie replied in a tone that suggested she was still less than convinced of the puffins' intelligence.

"So, what's our course to the Ice Dagger?" Soren asked.

"Due north. We shouldn't have any trouble spotting it, especially on a clear night like this. Ezylryb says it sticks straight out of the Everwinter Sea like a blade."

"I guess that's where they get the ice swords."

"So they say," Gylfie replied.

It was at the Ice Dagger that the Chaw of Chaws would split to perform their various tasks in the Northern Kingdoms before meeting up again. Before this, Soren and Gylfie had always been together on missions. But now, for the first time since they had known each other, they would soon be heading in opposite directions. It would be an odd feeling. But it could not be helped. They had each been given tasks specific to their particular talents.

"Ice Dagger, ho!" Twilight called out. A huge, jagged blade of ice sliced through the sea and stabbed the blackness of the night. Soren flew up to Twilight, who was flying point in the formation. "Will you look at that!" Twilight said, his voice full of wonder. "They say it never melts. That's why they can harvest those fantastic ice swords from it. Just think, Soren, what we could do with ice swords!"

Weapons, fighting, war in general — that was what occupied Twilight's mind most of the time. And he *was* a superb fighter. He could fight with anything, from a blazing branch and battle claws to his tongue, which was as fierce as any weapon when he unleashed his taunting verses, which were known to make an enemy go yeep and plunge to the ground. Having another weapon to contemplate — ice swords!— was almost more than Twilight's gizzard would be able to handle. Soren imagined that he could feel the twitches of Twilight's gizzard right now. *It's doing a little jig in there, I swear.*

It seemed impossible that on this sharp frozen blade that shot up from the sea, they could find a place to land, but there was a protuberance about a quarter of the way up that was almost like the hilt of a sword. It was there that they alighted.

The wind whipped around the icy blade that glimmered in the moonlight like a bewitched sea dagger thrust from the turbulent sea by some unseen water creature. Soren could almost imagine a claw beneath the surface gripping that blade. For the life of him, Soren could not figure out how other blades were made from the Ice Dagger, which seemed to him to be unbreakable. How could the owls of the Northern Kingdoms manage to pry off a piece to serve as a sword? It was also said that nothing was sharper than an ice sword, and that, properly taken care of, it would not melt even in the presence of fire.

Twilight could not stand still any longer and had begun to fly in circles around the Ice Dagger for a close examination. "I can see cracks where they might have pried off pieces. By Glaux, those edges look sharp. Gotta watch where you set down around here." His eyes were gleaming.

"Enough of that, Twilight. I have a few words to say before we split up." Soren coughed lightly and then faced the group. "We all know what we must do. And I know you shall all perform your tasks to the best of your abilities. Gylfie and Otulissa, you go directly from here to the Glauxian Sisters' retreat to deliver Dewlap, and then straight on to the Glauxian Brothers in the Bitter Sea. Ruby and Martin, you proceed to Stormfast Island, Ezylryb's birthplace, in the Bay of Kiel and find the Kielian snake called Hoke of Hock. Digger, Twilight, Eglantine, and I shall go to the Firth of Fangs to seek out Moss. After each group finishes its assigned task — whether it is research or petitioning for allies — we will then proceed to Dark Fowl Island. We will all meet there on the last night of the dwenking. Remember, you can't be late. Winter sets in early here. The katabatic winds drive the ice, and if the ice floes jam the channels and passages, we won't be able to tell the difference between an island and the mainland.

We'll be ice-locked. That's what they call it." The owls had all fallen silent, as if each one was imagining the terrible fate of being ice-locked, a prisoner of this frozen place.

Soren looked up at the sky. Clouds rolled over the moon, causing shadows to dance across the Ice Dagger. It sent a quiver through his gizzard. "This is full shine," he continued. "The last night of the dwenking, when we are to meet again, is fourteen nights from now." Soren looked at each of the owls standing before him on the hilt of the Ice Dagger. "So, good luck and Glauxspeed." He raised his wings, flapped once, twice, and lifted off into the night. Eglantine, Digger, and Twilight followed.

The battle claws of Ezylryb encasing Soren's talons sparkled fiercely in the moonlight. Once again, Ezylryb's words came back to Soren: *The claws are the keys to the Northern Kingdoms.*

So be it, Soren thought. *So be it.*

CHAPTER FOUR

A Circle of White Trees

Phew! I hope that is the last I ever see of that batty old owl," Otulissa said as they lifted into flight from the Glauxian Sisters' retreat. Dewlap had been left in the care of the Mother Superior. Gylfie had tried to say good-bye but Dewlap blinked at her with vacant, uncomprehending eyes. "We'll take good care of her, dear," the Mother Superior had said. "Don't worry."

Gylfie and Otulissa had tried to appear worried, but they weren't. They were simply relieved that this part of their mission was over. They carved two graceful arcs in the darkening sky under a spray of stars.

"I just can't wait to get to the Glauxian Brothers," Otulissa said. "Do you realize, Gylfie, that we are going to the very finest library in the entire owl universe?"

"Well, seeing as there are only three — ours at Ga'Hoole, St. Aggie's, and theirs — I don't think that's such a big deal."

"Oh, don't be that way."

"What way?" Gylfie shot back.

"You know. Just so . . . so negative," Otulissa muttered.

"I'm not negative, but it's just that I don't care how wonderful their library is. The way these owls live up here leaves something to be desired."

"You didn't like the burrows at the Glauxian Sisters' retreat."

"I'm not a Burrowing Owl."

"Well, neither are they. But what's one to do? There are no trees to speak of around here," Otulissa reasoned.

"Understatement of the year. I can't remember when I last saw a tree." Gylfie sighed rather mournfully.

"Most of the owls up here are Snowies. Snowies are used to ground living. At least, that's what I've read."

"Well, I'm not a Snowy, and I found our quarters at the Sisters' retreat less than comfortable." Gylfie looked down at the barren, ice-coated landscape below. *I am tree sick*, she thought. *How long has it been since I've slept in a tree?* She missed the Great Ga'Hoole Tree desperately. She missed the creaking of the timber in a fierce gale. She missed the stirring of the vines in a gentle summer breeze. She missed the spicy smell of the wood on a wet rainy day. She missed the moss of her own little nest in the hollow she shared with Soren and Digger and Twilight. She missed the port of the hollow that framed the sky, which was like the most beautiful but ever-changing painting. Sometimes there were clouds that cavorted like a herd of woolly creatures against the blue, and other times, as the sun was setting, the sky blazed with deep oranges and flaming pinks. Then clouds would stretch out and remind her of whales swimming through a fiery horizon at the edge of the world. Gylfie missed all of it. And to think that she had once upon a time lived not in a tree at all but in the hollow of a tall, prickly cactus in the desert. But that was so long ago that it almost seemed like make-believe, some story she had made up about a little Elf Owl who had lived happily in the Desert of Kuneer with her mum and da.

"Gylfie! Are you listening to me at all?" Otulissa was barking in her ear.

"Oh, sorry." She had stopped paying attention to Otulissa when the Spotted Owl had begun to run on about the library and the research she was planning to do and all the great intellects with whom she would have intense and wonderful discussions.

"I asked for a course check. You are the navigator, aren't you?"

"Yes, yes . . . let's see." Gylfie flipped her head almost completely around and then straight up. "Oh, Great Glaux!"

"What is it?"

"Just that–the Great Glaux constellation. We are, indeed, in the Northern Kingdoms. It's even more beautiful here. We never get to see it this time of year at the great tree." Gylfie's voice was full of wonder. "I am seeing constellations that Strix Struma only told us about. Look off to starboard, there — the Bear. Isn't it magnificent? And look at the stars in its paws. See how they are slightly green? And over there, just a bit to the south of it, is the crown of Hoole and . . ."

"But Hoole wore no crown," Otulissa interrupted. "Remember the legend? I've studied the entire cycle of the North Waters."

Oh, here she goes again. She's going to analyze a legend, Gylfie thought. Legends were made to be told and heard, not analyzed. And Gylfie knew this one by heart and gizzard. She would never forget it. At St. Aggie's, when Soren had whispered this legend in the glare of the moon-blaze chamber where they had been put for punishment, it had saved them. Legends cleared their minds and helped them resist the deadly glare of the moon in that white stone cell. Soren's voice came back to Gylfie now. *Once upon a time before there were kingdoms of owls, in a time of ever-raging wars, there was an owl hatched in the country of the Great North Waters and his name was Hoole. Some say there was an enchantment cast upon him at the time of his hatching, that he was given natural gifts of extraordinary power. But what was known of this owl was that he inspired other owls to great and noble deeds and that, although he wore no crown of gold, the owls knew him as a king, for indeed his good grace and conscience anointed him and his spirit was his crown.*

But while Gylfie had been looking up, Otulissa had been looking down.

"Look, Gylfie, trees!"

"Trees? Where?"

"Straight down there on that island."

"Why, we're here!" Gylfie cheered. "We're right on course for the Glauxian Brothers' retreat. That is the island. And there are tall, tall trees just like . . ."

"Yes, just like in the legend!" And Otulissa began to recite the story. "In a wood of straight tall trees he had hatched, in a glimmering time when the seconds slow between the last minute of the old year and the first of the new, and the forest on this night was sheathed in ice."

"Otulissa," Gylfie said slowly. "Are you thinking what I am thinking?"

"That this is the very place where Hoole was hatched?"

"These are the only trees we've seen since before the Ice Narrows."

"Gylfie, you must be right! And, of course, it makes perfect sense that the Glauxian Brothers would have their retreat here. . . . Why . . . why . . . Gylfie, they must have the original manuscripts. Oh! Oh, I can't wait! Oh, my brain might burst in anticipation!"

I doubt it, Gylfie thought to herself.

It was considered summer in the Northern Kingdoms. So the forest was not sheathed in ice as it was when Hoole had hatched. But still there were patches of snow on the ground. The first pink streaks of dawn were just washing across the sky. The trees were the straightest trees Gylfie had ever seen. They were fir trees and their needles and bark looked inky black against the pale dawn. They appeared to grow so thickly that, at first, the two owls wondered how they would ever pass through them. But they realized as they descended that the trees were not as close together as they had thought. Shafts of light pierced the forest and everything seemed to sparkle and glisten. The droplets of water on the needles refracted the light, splitting it up into countless little beams. It felt as though they were flying through a jeweled web of light and dew.

"How will we ever find the retreat?" Otulissa asked.

"Beats me," Gylfie replied.

"Well, you're the navigator."

"Flight navigator. The sky. The stars. Not land navigation." Gylfie swiveled her head, looking for any sign that might indicate where the Glauxian Brothers might dwell.

They flew on, lacing their way through the magical forest web. After nearly an hour, they came to a place where the trees thinned out and Gylfie spotted something ahead that intrigued her. "Let's land in that next tree," she whispered to Otulissa.

The two young owls perched on a slender branch. "Look over there," Gylfie whispered. Otulissa blinked. Through the fir trees were the whitest birch trees either one of them had ever seen. The trees grew in a circle, a perfect circle. And then, if one peered really hard, as Gylfie was now doing, there was something else.

"That's an owl," Gylfie whispered to Otulissa.

"Where? I don't see an owl."

"Over there, a few inches in front of that trunk." Gylfie pointed with one talon to indicate the tree she was looking at.

"I don't see —" Otulissa started to say, but then interrupted herself. "Wait. Great Glaux, it's a Snowy Owl."

And there was not just one Snowy but a half dozen standing sentry, their white plumage with the occasional dark spots blending in perfectly with the white-barked trees behind them. Gylfie and Otulissa had arrived at the retreat of the Glauxian Brothers.

CHAPTER FIVE
Firth of Fangs

T he name disturbs me," Digger said, looking down at the narrow finger of water they were following.

"What name?" Soren asked.

"This place where we are — the Firth of Fangs. Fangs ... well, you know — none of us has the fondest memories of them."

"Oh, that bobcat," Twilight replied dismissively. When the band of four had been on their long journey to the Great Ga'Hoole Tree, they had a most unfortunate encounter with a fiendishly ravenous bobcat. Digger, Soren, and Gylfie had never seen such long and horrible fangs. Twilight, however, claimed to have seen many in his day. Having been orphaned almost immediately after hatching, Twilight had brought himself up, taught himself how to fly, and lived a lifetime full of awesome danger and adventure almost before he had even molted his first set of feathers.

"*That* bobcat, you say? I seem to remember, Twilight,

that you didn't exactly find it a soothing experience," Soren spoke up now. Sometimes Soren found Twilight's complete denial of fear more irritating than his boasting.

"Not soothing, exactly," Twilight replied, "but I can't think of the word right now."

"Bracing, perhaps? Stimulating?" Digger said. "As in 'gets your blood going, sends a refreshing quiver through the old gizzard'?"

"Exactly. That's it!" Twilight replied, and Soren thought that Digger was sometimes just too nice.

"Well, let me tell you," Digger continued. "There is scant difference between a bracing feeling and a terrifying one. Fangs more than six inches long scare the be-Glaux out of me. And I cannot help but think that this Firth of Fangs place must have been named that for a reason. I only hope that the trip to seek out Moss, this old warrior friend of Ezylryb's, will be worth it."

"Well, Digger," Eglantine, who had been flying in between Twilight and the Burrowing Owl, began to speak quietly, "technically a firth is a long narrow body of water, an indentation in the seacoast."

"Good grief! If I didn't know better I would have thought it was Otulissa speaking. No, Eglantine, it's not the 'firth' part that bothers me. It's definitely the 'fang' part."

"But have you ever considered, Digger, that the firth

might be called a fang because it is long and curved like a fang?" Eglantine flew closer to him as she posed the question.

"Oh, that's a thought. Its shape . . ."

But before the Burrowing Owl could look to confirm this, Soren let loose with a gizzard-piercing shriek as only a Barn Owl can.

"What is it?" Digger said. But then they all saw where Soren was looking — straight down. Several late-summer ice floes that had broken off the winter pack ice bobbed peacefully in the waters of the firth. But from one ice floe, clearly visible in the moonlight, gushed a stream of blood. An immense white beast like none they had ever seen was tearing something apart. It tipped its head back. Its immense fangs were bright with blood, and in its claws it held the squirming body of a seal.

"Want to say hello to those fangs, Twilight?" Digger asked. "And with those claws it might provide a truly bracing experience!" The fangs were clearly longer than six inches.

Eglantine cried. "Look, I think that seal's baby is crying on the next floe! We've got to help that poor thing!"

"Mammish! Mammish!" wailed the small gray seal.

"We've gotta help!" Eglantine cried again. Soren's sister, Eglantine, the youngest and least experienced of all the owls, began a spiraling descent toward the floe where the baby seal wailed. The others followed. But by the time they arrived, she was already standing on the floe trying to calm the baby.

"It doesn't speak Hoolian, and I can't remember any Krakish," Eglantine said rather desperately.

"Umm, umm..." Soren was grasping for the proper Krakish words. How he wished Otulissa were here. She was the only one who was fluent. The rest of them could manage only a few choppy phrases and random words. But Soren began. "Baby be all right! Baby be all right!" He looked around anxiously. The flow of blood from the seal's mother had dyed the water around them red. Twilight was transfixed. "I think it's a bear — a white bear."

"A *polar* bear?" Digger asked.

"Yes, that's it, I think," Twilight said.

"Oh, Great Glaux," Digger sighed. "Now we know why this place is called the Firth of Fangs. I've read that polar bears are the biggest carnivores on Earth."

"And we are a floating meat market here," Soren said tensely as the floe with the bear drifted closer and closer.

"They are swimmers, too — powerful swimmers," Digger said with a tremor in his voice.

"But can they fly?" Twilight said. "I suggest we get out of here quickly."

"But what about the baby?" Eglantine said in a pleading voice. The baby was now making quite a racket. "We can't leave the baby." Eglantine was crying almost as hard as the baby seal.

Suddenly, there was a tremendous bump and the owls and the seal skidded to the other edge of the ice floe. The polar bear's floe had crashed into them. The bear stopped gorging for the moment and lifted its face. In the moonlight it was an awesome sight. Its pure white muzzle was now stained with blood. It tipped its head back. *"Arrrrraggggh!"* It was a roar that shook the ice, the sea, not to mention the owls' gizzards.

No translation needed, Soren thought. They had to get out of here. They had to save themselves. The baby seal was a lost cause. He raised his wings and began to flap them. The others did as well. All except for Eglantine, who staunchly stood her ground — or rather her ice — on her freezing-cold talons.

"Eglantine, fly up here this minute. That's an order," Soren shreed down at her.

"I'm not going to leave her, Soren. I'm not."

"Eglantine, I am the commander of this mission. You have to do what I say."

"I don't care if you are the commander, Soren. I know what it's like to be left behind and all alone. I'm staying."

"Eglantine, we cannot endanger the entire mission for the sake of one baby seal."

"I'm not going to leave her, Soren. I won't. I don't care if you are the boss." Soren looked down at Eglantine as she stood firmly on the ice floe. She had grown stronger in every way since recovering from her shattering by the Pure Ones.

By this time the bear had ceased to eat. He seemed to be looking back and forth between Soren, who flew in circles above the two ice floes, and Eglantine, who stood next to the baby seal. He dipped one enormous paw into the sea and commenced to wash his muzzle, then brushed off some seal hair that had fallen on his chest. Soren, Twilight, and Digger heard him mumble something, or perhaps it was more like a rumble. They looked down in horror as they saw Eglantine stepping closer to the edge of the ice floe. The bear had slipped off his piece of ice and had placed his huge paw on the edge of the floe where Eglantine stood. "Get back, Eglantine! Get back!"

"Fly, you fool!" Twilight screamed.

"Eglantine, have you gone yoicks?" Digger shouted.

"Shut up, the lot of you!" she screamed. Then she tipped her head back and nosed her beak closer to the muzzle of the polar bear.

At this point Soren went yeep. Never in his life had he

gone yeep, but how could he lose his only sister after all he had gone through to save her? He had saved her from the Pure Ones twice already. "But that is a polar bear, for Glaux's sake!" he cried, and recovered his wing power a foot from the ice floe. So he did not crash but set down gently some distance from his sister and out of the reach of the bear.

Eglantine turned to Soren and in a patronizing voice said, "He says he doesn't eat babies."

"Oh, so all of a sudden you speak Krakish, do you?" Soren challenged his sister and took a small step forward.

"Few words speak sister . . . me speak little bit Hoole." The polar bear raised his other huge paw, which had been underwater and, with the longest, deadliest claws Soren had ever seen, tried to indicate the "little bit" of Hoole he spoke by holding together his pinky claw with his first claw. It was a gizzard-freezing sight. Meanwhile, Eglantine pressed on, and Soren listened to one of the oddest conversations he had ever heard.

"Phawish prak nraggg grash m'whocki," said the polar bear.

"You don't say?" said Eglantine.

Does she really understand all this or is she just pretending? I bet she's pretending, Soren thought. "What's he saying, Eglantine?"

"Uh, it's something about lemmings and . . ."

"And mice and all things owl eats," rumbled the polar bear.

"Huh?" said Soren. He blinked in amazement. Eglantine had understood some of this.

"Ja! Ja! Ja!" The polar bear was nodding his head and saying yes in Krakish. To do this he dropped his jaws wide open. His mouth was as big as a tree hollow. Four owls could have easily fit in it. "I no tell owl what to eat. Rodents disgusting, snake never. You no tell polar bear what to eat. Mishnacht?"

"Mishnacht means 'understand,' Soren," Eglantine said primly. "You do understand, don't you?" she said in a tone that was really beginning to annoy Soren. Eglantine then turned to the polar bear. "Yes, we mishnacht."

"Gunda, gunda!" the bear replied.

Before Eglantine could translate Soren said, "That means 'good, good.'"

"And I eat no babies."

"No babies, right," Soren said.

"No owls, either?" Digger asked. He was hovering above the bear at a safe distance.

"Nachsun! *Blahhh!*" He made a throw-up sound in the back of his huge throat. "Owls no blubber. Feathers disgusting!"

"Yes, quite," Digger replied and flew off.

The bear focused now on Soren. Suddenly, the ice floe tipped at a precarious angle. Soren and Eglantine began a precipitous slide toward the polar bear. Eglantine smacked right against his muzzle still stained with the seal's blood despite having been washed in the seawater.

"Eglantine! Fly!" Soren screeched. She did, as did Soren.

"A millimeter! I swear you missed those jaws by a millimeter." Digger was gasping.

Meanwhile, the polar bear, still resting his elbows on the ice floe, scratched his head and looked up. "Hvrash g'mear mclach? Where you go? I say I no eat owls. You good owls. I see dat owl wear claws of Lyze. Lyze of Kiel. You know Lyze of Kiel?"

"Do *you* know Lyze of Kiel?" Soren replied in astonishment. *Ezylryb!* Soren thought. *He knows Ezylryb!*

"I know the Lyze of Kiel? What question is dat? Grachunn naghish prahnorr gundamyrr Lyze effen Kiel erraggh frisen gunda yo macht leferzundt."

"It sounds like he's gargling with rocks," Twilight said.

All four owls were now hovering slightly closer to the polar bear's head.

"Are you following any of this, Eglantine?" Soren asked.

"Not exactly. But frisen gunda means 'good friend.'"

"Ja, ja," the bear was saying. "Good friend is Lyze. Me commander of ice troops during War of Ice Claws."

"Ice troops?" Twilight said with sudden interest.

"Ja. We keep ice floes guarded. Lyze and Glauxspeed unit rearm and refuel on our floes. And old Moss's unit — the Frost Beaks, too."

"Moss! You know Moss?" Soren cried.

This set off another gush of Krakish, by which the owls understood that this immense white bear streaked with blood did indeed know Moss, and had no interest in devouring them.

The owls lighted down on the floe. "Are you are saying," Soren stepped up close to the bear, "that you will lead us to where Moss lives in the Bay of Fangs?"

"Ja."

Those teeth, those fangs, they are as long as I am tall! Soren tried not to tremble as he spoke. "That would be most kind of you."

"Ja, I try to be kind." He looked around and wiped his muzzle again. "Eating seal not mean. Eat just to live. You eat rat, mouse, lemmings just to live. I must eat to live, too. Right? "

"Yes, exactly," said Digger stepping forward. "Tell us now, what is your name?"

"Svallborg. But you can call me Svall."

"Good, or rather, gunda. And I am Digger and this is Soren and his sister, Eglantine, and Twilight here. We will follow your lead from the air."

"Gunda! Gunda. Framisch longha," Svallborg said, and then in one long graceful movement shoved himself from the ice floe. The owls rose in the air to follow Svall. He was a beautiful sight. The owls had never imagined that such an enormous animal could move with such grace. Paddling with his front paws and barely making a splash, Svall moved through the water at an amazing speed.

Eglantine could not help but look back at the baby seal. She saw it slip off the ice floe and swim toward a swirl of water where small silver fish were schooling. *Hmmm . . . ,* thought Eglantine, *maybe she's a little older than I figured.* Just then the seal dived and seconds later came up with a fish flopping in her mouth.

What will Moss be like? Soren wondered as they flew above the great bear. Ezylryb had said that the claws would be his passport, his safe-conduct permit. But there was a burden that came with the claws as well. What would these owls of the Northern Kingdoms expect from him? What was he supposed to be? Would they think him worthy of the claws? Would they think he was some sort of imposter? And worst of all, he was coming here to ask these owls who had lived in peace for years to join in another battle. What would they think of him and of the cause for which he had been sent?

It was not exactly fear that Soren was experiencing, but with each stroke of his wings in this vast, frozen, and desolate land he began to feel smaller and smaller and less and less worthy. He looked down at his talons, which were armed in the battle claws of Ezylryb. They glimmered dark and mocking in the light of the moon. They were no heavier than his regular battle claws, but they had seen more action in one owl's life than twenty ordinary owl lifetimes. They carried the burden of history and the weight of a true hero — Ezylryb. It seemed absurd to Soren that he was wearing these claws. With each stroke, each wing beat, they seemed heavier and heavier. But he must go on; not only go on, he must lead. There was no turning back and yet going forward seemed so very, very hard.

Agony! Sheer agony, Soren thought.

CHAPTER SIX

The Retreat of the Glauxian Brothers

O tulissa was experiencing a different kind of agony from that which Soren felt. No one had ever mentioned to her that the Glauxian Brothers were bound in a vow of silence.

Silence! Who ever heard of such a stupid thing? How can one have an intellectual conversation if one takes a vow of silence? This was the one-sided conversation that thundered incessantly in Otulissa's brain. She and Gylfie could speak only in the small hollow they shared together. There was no talking at meals. In the library, all requests for books were made in writing. Even the nest-maid snakes, generally very chatty by nature, were silent. Otulissa was completely frinked. Oh, yes, there were certain times when one could speak — discussions could be held in study hollows, which were off the library. But some of the most stimulating and intellectual discussion that Otulissa had ever had were in the dining hollow of the Great Ga'Hoole Tree over a nice, plump roasted vole. And here, that was impossible.

Gylfie, on the other hand, found it a relief to have Otulissa bound to enforced silence. She saw that there was a kind of beauty in this silence. The brothers of the Glauxian retreat were more alive and interesting than any owls she had ever encountered — in their own way. She saw that actually there was a kind of communication among them, but one had to be keen to an array of subtle signs and signals to notice it. Words — at least, spoken words — were not always needed. She tried to explain this to Otulissa, but to no avail.

"But you don't understand, Gylfie. This library is the most magnificent I could have ever imagined. And I am finding out so much about fleckasia, but I need to talk about it, too. Not only fleckasia, but things called cold fire and ice flames. Sort of the opposite of bonk flames."

"Well, there are those times in the study hollows."

"I know, but I can't get a word in edgewise." Otulissa sighed.

"What? You, of all owls, can't get a word in edgewise?"

"You don't understand. These owls are weird. They don't talk much. But they have these odd ways of communicating *without talking* and even in the study hollows, where they are allowed to talk, there is a lot of silence.

There are these gaps in the conversation, but it's still like they are talking. And I can't get in on it."

"Hmmm" was all Gylfie could say. She didn't know quite what to tell her. Poor Otulissa — the most fluent in Krakish of all the owls of the Chaw of Chaws All those irregular verbs she had practiced on the flight north, and no place to use them.

"Look, Otulissa, I'll go to a study hollow with you and see if I can help."

"Oh, would you, Gylfie? That would be so great. I mean, I've been reading all this stuff about fleckasia but I need to discuss it. And they also have the most complete history of the War of the Ice Claws and other wars, too. I need to study the strategy, you know, for the invasion plan of St. Aggie's. After all, it is my plan that we are going to use and that was why I was sent here by the parliament. They're counting on us, Gylfie."

Us; she said "us." Gylfie supposed it was nice of Otulissa to include her. But it was Otulissa's plan that the owls of Ga'Hoole were most likely to implement in the coming invasion. The Chaw of Chaws was not here in the Northern Kingdoms solely to recruit owls to fight, as Soren was doing in the Firth of Fangs, but to study the strategies of invasion.

If this invasion did indeed take place, it would be the

largest in the history of owlkind — staggering in size, epic in significance. In one night, thousands of owls of all kinds would cross seventy leagues from the Island of Hoole to the canyonlands of St. Aegolius Academy for Orphaned Owls. The land of this region was cut by deep ravines. It bristled with rocky spires and needles. It appeared barren of trees, rivers, or lakes. But it was rich in one thing: the deadly flecks that could destroy owls' minds.

St. Aggie's had fallen and was now held by the most dangerous owls on earth, the Pure Ones. The Pure Ones were smart. They knew enough about flecks to be able to destroy any owls that flew against them and challenged their plan for complete dominion over the owl universe.

Only a massive invasion of the canyonlands could finish their tyranny forever. It would be an invasion requiring the help of many allies. And the very best of these allies were to be found in the Northern Kingdoms. Otulissa had been given the task of studying all she could about fleckasia and the battle strategies implemented during the War of the Ice Claws. And the best place to do that was here in the magnificent library of the Glauxian Brothers' retreat.

Life at the retreat followed a fairly unvarying routine. The hours of the night were spent in meditative flight rather than practicing the kinds of skills that were constantly being honed at the Great Ga'Hoole Tree. The brothers traded knowledge and their skills with herbs for live coals from rogue colliers. They rotated hunting chores and had no real need for navigation since they rarely left the region of their retreat. Gylfie was eternally grateful that the brothers' retreat was not underground like the Glauxian Sisters' but in the hollows of the ring of birch trees. The evening meal, tweener, was always followed by several hours of meditative flight. When the brothers returned to the retreat, they broke up into the study hollows to pursue their scholarly interests in herbs, literature, and science.

The silence in the dining hollow on this particular evening was as thick as ever. As Otulissa and Gylfie entered they noticed once again a very peculiar-looking old Whiskered Screech huddled in a corner eating with the help of nurselike attendants, a Short-eared Owl and an elderly Kielian snake who was constantly flicking up some sort of dark red juice from a goblet with his forked tongue. Gylfie was not sure why the snake stuck so close to the old Whiskered Screech. But both Gylfie and Otulissa had noticed that on the meditative flights the Short-eared Owl accompanied the old owl. Gylfie felt there was something vaguely familiar about the decrepit old one, but she could not figure out what. Apparently, the code of silence was not always practiced with this owl, for

Gylfie often saw the attendant whispering something in his ear. She supposed that perhaps, for the frail and elderly, exceptions were permitted. However, she had never seen the owl speak a word in response. Indeed, the old thing seemed to be lost in a daze, his yellow eyes permanently set on some invisible horizon. The more she saw of this old owl, the more he reminded her of someone. She decided that tonight she would try to fly near him and his attendants during the meditation flight.

In the meantime, Otulissa's attention had been drawn elsewhere — to a handsome young Spotted Owl. He was quite attractive and flew with great style, and she had thought she might try to fly near him. *Fat lot of good it will do me if I can't even talk,* she thought. *Might as well forget it. It would only be a distraction.* She hadn't come here to socialize, but to learn. And he probably didn't know that much, anyway. She was certain he had arrived only a few days before she and Gylfie did.

After tweener, thirty owls or more rose in the crisp night air of the forest where Hoole had been hatched and began their nighttime meditation. The flight formation was a loose circle of owls that resembled the circle of the birch trees of the retreat. There was ample space between each one so that every owl could meditate without distraction. All owls were known for their silent flight, but these owls of the retreat flew in a silence more complete than either Gylfie or Otulissa had ever experienced.

During this particular flight, Otulissa had chosen as her subject of meditation the legends of Hoole. She was trying to imagine what this forest had been like when the great owl had hatched in that glimmering time in the icy forest, when the seconds had slowed between the last minute of the old year and the first of the new. She was startled when she heard the air nearby ruffle with a stir of wings and then next to her a Spotted Owl slipped in. Not *a* Spotted Owl, but *the* Spotted Owl.

"The silence is sort of getting to me," he whispered.

Otulissa's head nearly spun around entirely. She blinked in astonishment.

"Oh, go on, tell me you don't like to talk," he said. "I can spot a talker a league away." He sent a riffle through his pinfeathers, a special trick Spotted Owls did that showed off their spots magnificently.

Otulissa tried to repress a churr. *Oh, how glorious!* she thought. *Words, language!* "Aren't we breaking the rules?" she whispered.

"They don't really have hard-and-fast rules here, exactly. You're supposed to learn them — gradually. They don't have any real rhot gorts, either."

"You mean flint mops?" Otulissa asked, for she was not sure of the Krakish words for the Ga'Hoole term for "punishment," which was flint mop.

"Yes, that's it in Hoolian. But you speak pretty good Krakish."

"Oh, a little trouble with the passive subjunctive in irregular verbs, but thank you," Otulissa said modestly and blinked in her most fetching manner.

"What's your name?" he asked.

"Otulissa," she replied.

"Otulissa," the owl said reflectively. "A very traditional name."

Otulissa felt a tingle of joy in her gizzard. Here was an owl of her station, of her background. He recognized that Spotted Owl females were often called by the ancient and distinguished name of Otulissa.

"And what is your name, if I may ask?"

"Of course. I am Cleve of Firthmore."

"Cleve of Firthmore!" Otulissa gasped. "The Firthmore Passage in the Tridents?"

The owl nodded in reply.

Otulissa's eyes were blinking madly as she flew. "From the royal hollow of Snarth?" Once more, the owl called Cleve nodded. "Then you are a prince. For that is where the clan of Krakor comes from." *And*, thought Otulissa, *the* clan of Krakor is the oldest and most aristocratic clan in the land of the Great North Waters. It was, in fact, the clan for which the Krakish language of the Northern Kingdoms was named. This was a clan of words, of stories, of legends. They were writers and tellers of history, of literature. It was the clan of her beloved Strix Struma and her cherished Strix Emerilla, the renowned weathertrix of the last century whose books Otulissa had intellectually devoured.

"What are you doing here at the retreat?" Otulissa asked. "Is it a custom for royalty to come here?"

"Not exactly. I really came because . . . well, how to put it? Much of my study back in the Tridents has been military. And there hasn't been a war for years now. The War of the Ice Claws was over long ago."

"Yes, but don't you think military knowledge is still useful?" Otulissa whispered. A slightly wary tone had crept into her voice.

"Not really," Cleve replied casually, as if he might be commenting on the weather. "You see, I came here to study medicine. Quite frankly, I don't believe in war — ever."

"You what?" Otulissa shrieked.

"Please, dear." A Snowy Owl had flown up. "This is a meditation flight. Some whispering perhaps, but shouting? Oh, no, we can't have that," the Snowy said gently and flew off.

Just at that moment, Gylfie also experienced a shock, and Otulissa's cry was like an exclamation point in the night, punctuating a most startling revelation: *Ifghar! That is what the Short-eared Owl had just called the frail old Whiskered Screech! Impossible!* Gylfie told herself. She caught an updraft so she could fly directly beneath them. Of course, there was mostly silence, but occasionally the Short-eared Owl found it necessary to redirect the Whiskered Screech's flight path and, in whispered tones, she would nudge him back on course. "Now, now, old dear, stroke with that port wing. It's getting stronger." There was a low grumble. "No need for that, Ifghar. You can do it, dear. You can."

Gylfie blinked and felt her gizzard grow heavy. *How could this be? Ezylryb's turnfeather brother here?!* This, indeed, was something to meditate on. Then came that shriek from Otulissa. And the next thing Gylfie knew, Otulissa was flying beside her.

"It really frinks me off! I can't believe it, and him coming from the royal hollow of Snarth in the Tridents. Shameful! Absolutely shameful."

"Sssh!" The Short-eared Owl flying attendance for Ifghar shushed her from above.

Gylfie had no idea what Otulissa was beaking off about. But she and Otulissa definitely had to talk. Forget study hollow and discussions on fleckasia and disorders of the gizzard! Gylfie had to tell Otulissa about Ifghar. The only reason that she and Digger and Soren knew about Ifghar, the treacherous brother of Ezylryb, was because Octavia, Ezylryb's nest-maid snake, had told them. She told them about Lil, the Whiskered Screech that both Ezylryb and his brother had fallen in love with. But Lil had preferred Ezylryb and had taken him as her mate. Both brothers served as commanders in the Glauxspeed artillery unit during the War of the Ice Claws. Ifghar was so incensed by Lil's refusal and so jealous of Ezylryb that he became a turnfeather and betrayed not just his brother but the entire Kielian League to the enemy, the League of the Ice Talons. Lil and Ezylryb made a fierce combat team, and Ifghar swore to the commander of the Ice Talons that with his help they could defeat them. He then had planned to capture Lil for his own.

Gylfie couldn't wait to get back to the hollow to tell Otulissa. *Ifghar here!* Ezylryb's treacherous brother. It was unbelievable.

CHAPTER SEVEN
Flivling and Riffles

"But Ifghar's plan went terribly wrong for everyone." Gylfie sighed.

"How so?" Otulissa asked. They had returned from the meditation flight and were in their own hollow, high in one of the birch trees. The wind had picked up and the birches, which were quite slender compared to the Great Ga'Hoole Tree, swayed wildly in the night. Both Gylfie and Otulissa enjoyed the movement. It gave them the odd sensation of still flying abroad in the dark folds of the evening sky while at the same time being cozy in their hollow.

"Lil was killed in the battle," Gylfie replied. "It was in that same battle that Ezylryb lost one of his talons, and Octavia was blinded."

"Are you sure that scruffy old owl is Ifghar?" Otulissa asked. Gylfie nodded.

"What's he doing here?"

"The League of the Ice Talons was finally defeated long after Ezylryb and Octavia had come here and then left for the great tree. I guess by that time Ifghar was pretty old and had nowhere to go. He certainly couldn't fly back to the Kielian League. Turnfeathers are hardly welcomed guests. And the Glauxian Brothers are always neutral, so it was a safe haven for him. But I would sure like to ask his attendant, the Short-eared Owl, some questions, though."

"Good luck," Otulissa said.

"Oh, they aren't always that strict about the silence thing. It's mostly in the public spaces of the retreat. I'm sure I could go to her hollow and have a little chat. But what happened to *you* tonight, Otulissa? You certainly broke the silence."

Otulissa sighed deeply. "It's a long story. I'll make it short. Extremely handsome owl who happens to be a prince. And yoicks."

Gylfie blinked. "A prince who's yoicks?"

"Oh, he has this totally yoickish notion. He doesn't believe in war. Can you imagine, Gylfie?"

"Well, I don't find that hard to understand at all. I mean, when Ezylryb came here to the retreat, he hung up his battle claws and gave up fighting."

"But this owl is a prince, Gylfie. A prince from the royal hollow of Snarth of the Trident Islands in Firthmore. Do you know their history? The battles they fought? It's the same hollow that Strix Struma came from."

"Well, he doesn't believe in war. That's all," Gylfie said.

"That's all?" Otulissa shot back. "I don't see it that way."

"Well, what does he believe in?"

"Medicine. He came here to study herbs and healing."

"The Glauxian Brothers are experts in the healing arts. They have the biggest collection of books on medicine, herbs, and all manner of diseases anywhere. That's why we're here, remember? So you can read the only existing copy of *Fleckasia and Other Disorders of the Gizzard*."

"I know, I know," Otulissa said testily. "So we better get going because we've probably already missed a good bit of the study hollow's near-wordless discussion. I tell you, this place frinks me off."

Gylfie blinked her eyes rapidly. Otulissa could be simply impossible. "Look, just promise me one thing?" she asked.

"What's that?"

"No more outbursts! The next thing you know, you'll be saying the you-know-what word."

"I won't. Don't be ridiculous."

But Otulissa could be unpredictable. *Like right now,* Gylfie thought. It was clear to her that Otulissa had really liked the handsome Spotted Owl. That was so unlike Otulissa. She had no time for such things, and Glaux knew she wouldn't know the first thing about flivling, the owl word for flirting.

How wrong one can be! Gylfie thought as she observed Otulissa in the study hollow. A discussion of fleckasia had been under way for some time. Of course, leading the conversation was Otulissa, carrying on about the four quadrants of the gizzard and the humors associated with each of these quadrants. And to whom was she tipping and cocking her head as she made her remarks? None other than Cleve of Firthmore, prince of the royal hollow of Snarth.

"For example, Cleve." Blink, blink went Otulissa's eyes with a sparkle that Gylfie had never seen before. "I would say that you have an abundance of fleebis in your third quadrant."

"Really!" replied Cleve.

"Really!" Otulissa said. "Many of the brightest and most perceptive Spotted Owls are known for this. For example, a distant relative of mine, the renowned weather-trix of the last century, Strix Emerilla —"

"Aaahhhhh!" the owls all opened their beaks in recognition of the eminent scholar's name.

Gylfie could not believe what she was witnessing. Great Glaux, it could wreck the mission if Otulissa — Otulissa of all owls — was distracted! And all because of some frinking prince from snape of Snarth — or wherever. And was that a riffle she saw passing through from Otulissa's pinfeathers and lighting up those pale tawny spots of hers to their best advantage? *Oh, Glaux-in-a-box! She's gone yoicks right down to her pinfeathers!*

CHAPTER EIGHT
Hoke of Hock

"I have never in my life met animals as tight-beaked as these creatures of Stormfast Island," Martin was muttering to himself as he and Ruby flew over the westernmost edge of Stormfast, scouring the landscape below for the kind of terrain where an elderly Kielian snake might dwell. The Kielian snakes were a peculiar breed, at least from an owl's point of view. To begin with, they ranged in colors from pale greenish-blue to turquoise. They were not blind and were known for their incredible muscles and their fantastic industry. They were also unbelievably supple. This, combined with their muscle power, allowed them to penetrate places unreachable by other snakes, actually tunnelling into enemy territory. They could move earth, even frozen earth! And they could swim as well as any seal or polar bear.

It was Ezylryb who had seen how useful these snakes could be in war. He had come up with the idea for a stealth force of Kielian snakes that would fight both on the ground and in the air on the backs of owls. Hoke of Hock had been the supreme commander of this stealth unit. Octavia had trained under him. And now Martin and Ruby had been sent to recruit him for the war against the Pure Ones. A division of Kielian snakes was a crucial part of the plan for the invasion of the canyonlands.

But there was a problem. Hoke of Hock seemed to have utterly vanished and none of the other Kielian snakes or owls on Stormfast were inclined to say much about him. Ruby and Martin had first flown to the promontory called Hock. But there was no trace of the old snake. And now once again they were flying over the ragged promontory of the island that jutted out into the turbulent waters of this wind-lashed shore where he supposedly lived. They didn't have much time. In a few nights they were due to rendezvous on Dark Fowl Island with the other owls of the Chaw of Chaws.

"It's going to be terribly embarrassing if we are the only owls who don't do our part," Martin said.

"Yeah," Ruby replied. "I'm sure Otulissa has done hers and more."

"She's probably found that book, memorized it, and four others besides."

"Well, if we don't find this snake before we meet up with the rest, maybe we can ask them to help us," Ruby said in a hopeful voice.

"You forget we have a deadline. Pack ice, the katabatic winds."

"Ohhh!" groaned Ruby. "I did forget. Pack ice sounds worse that getting mobbed by crows."

"It's not the ice so much as the katabatic winds that drive the pack ice. We don't want to have to beat against those to get home."

"Kind of like getting stuck in the rim of a hurricane's eye, I guess," Ruby said with quiet dread in her voice. Getting stuck in a hurricane's eye rim was just about the worst thing Ruby and Martin could imagine. If this happened, an owl would spin around violently forever and ever, the force of the wind tearing off its wings and stripping every feather from its body. It was a terrible way to die.

"Look, I see something down there," Martin said suddenly.

"Where?" asked Ruby.

"Straight down. It looks like a glimmering —"

"I see it!"

The two young owls began a dizzying spiral descent. A sinuous glowing streak oozed slowly over the ground. They hovered, almost mesmerized by the undulating movement. Suddenly, the streak coiled up, waved its large bulbous head, and opened a mouth showing long, very sharp fangs. "Vasshink derkuna framachtin?"

"Ruby, what's the word for 'little' in Krakish?"

"You asking me?"

"'Michten,' I think that's it," Martin said and then began to speak to the snake. "Iby bisshen michten Krakish."

"Hoolish fynn? Vhor issen?"

"Uh . . . uh . . . yeah. We're from Ga'Hoole, the great tree."

"Bisshen michten Hoolian, erkutzen. Speak me little Hoolian."

Martin looked at Ruby. "I think we'd better land."

As the two owls alighted on the rocky promontory, the snake, still coiled, said, "Gunden vhagen."

Martin tipped his head. "Gunden vhagen." Ruby, watching Martin, did the same and mumbled the Krakish words for good evening.

"Vhrunk tuoy achtin?"

"Huh?" Martin said. "I mean, pardon."

"What comes you here for?"

"Oh . . . oh, yes . . . uh . . . uh . . . just a minute. Hold on." Martin turned to Ruby. "Get out that word sheet Otulissa made up for us."

Ruby untied a slender metal tube from her leg and then drew out a piece of paper.

"What's the word for snake?" Martin muttered with exasperation.

"Hordo!" the snake said.

"Yes," replied Martin. "Exactly. You are a hordo."

The serpent slid his eyes in contempt. They glittered in an unnerving way. "I know I am snake. Vhat you tink, me stupid?"

"You're a Kielian snake."

"Ja, ja."

"I mean . . . maybe you know this other Kielian snake we look for. His name is Hoke of Hock."

"Why you need Hoke of Hock?"

Well, at least he's chattier than the other creatures we've met, Martin thought.

"You good flier, Short-eared."

"You've been watching us?" Martin said in a wary voice.

"Ja, ja."

"For how long?" Ruby asked.

"Two days, maybe three," the snake replied.

"And you — Northern Saw-whet, you spiral dive like . . . oh, cominzee bisshen?" It was obvious that the snake was searching for a word he needed. ". . . Like . . . like a coal diver."

Martin blinked. "You mean, like a colliering owl?"

"That's it. Ja, ja, colliering owl."

Martin stepped closer to the snake. Northern Saw-whet Owls were small, and even stretching himself up as tall as he could, Martin was still shorter than the coiled snake. But he wanted the snake to pay attention to him. "You're Hoke, aren't you? You're the Kielian snake that Ezylryb sent us to find."

"Maybe, maybe not."

"Yes, you are. And you speak better Hoolian than we speak Krakish. You understand a lot. Why have you been hiding from us — and just now hiding how much you understand?"

"How I know Ezylryb really sent you? How I know who you are or who you pretend to be?" the snake demanded to know.

"We don't *pretend* to be anything," Ruby said huffily.

"I give test," the snake replied. "Who is Ezylryb's nestmaid?"

"Octavia!" both owls answered at once.

"How many talons does Ezylryb have on port foot?"

"Three," Martin and Ruby both cried out.

"Hmmm." The snake waved its head as if trying to think of a harder question. "All right. I got one."

Ruby's and Martin's gizzards began to tremble slightly. What if they missed this question?

"Ready?"

"Ready!" they both answered.

"Vhat be that old Whiskered Screech's favorite weather song? He always sing in dirty weather."

"We know that!" Ruby lofted into the air with glee and began singing.

> *We are the owls of the weather chaw*
> *We take it blistering*
> *We take it all*
>
> *Roiling boiling gusts*
> *We're the owls with the guts*

By the time she got to the second verse, the snake was wagging his head to the beat. It was a robust, irresistible song.

"Sound almost as good in Hoolian as Krakish!" the snake said. Soon, all three creatures, the two owls and the old Kielian snake, were roaring the song. The owls lofted into short merry flights; the snake oozed and swirled himself into the unbelievable contortions of an ancient Kielian snake dance.

> *For blizzards our gizzards*
> *do tremble with joy*

An ice storm, a gale, how we love blinding hail
We fly forward and backward
Upside down and flat
Do we flinch? Do we wail?
Do we skitter or scutter?
No! We yarp one more pellet
and fly straight for the gutter!
Do we screech? Do we scream?
Do we gurgle? Take pause?
Not on your life!
For we are the best
of the best of the chaws.

Finally, as the last verse drew to a close, the snake coiled up again, waved his head in a most graceful manner and said, "You are right. I am Hoke of Hock. Now, what does my old commander want? You know, of course, I flew with his beloved mate, Lil."

"You flew with Lil?" Ruby said with awe.

"Oh, yes," Hoke replied softly. "I was with her when she died."

Martin and Ruby had followed the Kielian snake to his "nost," as he called the small rocky cavern that the snakes lived in. It was fairly roomy, so the three creatures fit in comfortably. But the roar of the sea pounding on the rocks was tremendous, and they had to shout to be heard.

"But how come you didn't die?" Ruby asked.

"Because I swim. Lil went down into the sea, in deep, deep water. I try so hard to rescue her. . . ." Hoke shook his head wearily. "I do not have words to tell how hard I tried." He wept a strange glittery fluid.

Martin hopped over to Hoke and gave his turquoise scales a small pat.

"Takk, takk," the snake said, nodding his head. "Thank you. Thank you."

"Gare heeldvig," Martin replied, which meant in Krakish "think nothing of it."

"Hey, hey," said the old snake a little more cheerfully. "You learning to bisshen good Krakish, but now young'uns, you tell me vhat my old friend Ezylryb needs."

Martin and Ruby took turns explaining. But as Martin drew to a close he had the distinct feeling that Hoke was not convinced. He was going to have to plead harder, let out all the stops. Martin gulped.

"Look, the coming battle is not just a matter of life and death for the owls of Ga'Hoole but for all the owl kingdoms. . . . It could even affect snakes, all snakes, Kielian and others. I don't know if I can explain how deadly these flecks are. It's not just that creatures die from them. To simply die would be *easy*." Martin noticed a new alertness in Hoke. "It's that the flecks have the power to make us mindless tools in the talons of the most evil owls in the history of owlkind. And, as we speak, the Pure Ones are learning how to use the largest supply of flecks on Earth." Martin finally stopped. He looked at Hoke.

Hoke sighed. "Vhat you say is frightening but you see before you a very old snake. Too old to go into battle. But, yes, I could perhaps raise a battalion or two of owls and snakes and help in training them. But it must be agreed to by the parliament. Perhaps not the training but our going. The parliament will decide that. We are tired of war. You must understand."

"Yes, we understand." Martin nodded. "The War of the Ice Claws was so long. But you say a battalion or two?"

The snake nodded.

Martin knew they would need more, much more. Ezylryb was hoping for a regiment. Now Martin would have to ask the question he dreaded. "You realize it's an invasion? We'll need more than two battalions. Do you suppose you could train nest-maid snakes?"

In one swift flash of turquoise, Hoke coiled up. "Are you yoicks?! Yes, I know Hoolian word for crazy. Same in Krakish. Yoicks. Nest-maids? You two drop your brains in the sea?"

"Just asking," Martin said in a small voice. "You know, they are hard workers."

"They're weak. They have no muscle. And they're silly, too! Nunchat! Nachsun, Nynik, Nuftan!" Which basically meant "no, never, no way" in Krakish.

"All right. All right. Don't worry about it. Forget I said anything about nest-maids. Gare heeldvig," Martin replied quickly. Hoke relaxed and began to uncoil again. "Tell me something," Martin said, trying to change the subject, but also asking out of genuine curiosity, "whatever happened to Ezylryb's brother, Ifghar?"

"The turnfeather?" Hoke spat out the words.

"Yes."

"He was wounded pretty badly himself. He went off with the League of the Ice Talons with his turnscale snake, Gragg."

"A Kielian snake?"

"Ja, ja. Miserable piece of serpent if there ever was one. Liked his bingle juice too much."

"Bingle juice?"

"Ja, ja. You know, can make one trufynkken." Hoke wobbled his head around.

"Oh!" Martin and Ruby said at once. Bingle juice was like the Ga'Hoole berry wine the older owls sometimes drank at festivals.

"Ja, that snake go with anyone who give him a drink. That's why he kept with Ifghar. Don't know where they went. I think the Ice Talons League finally threw him out. Nobody trusts a turnfeather or a turnscale."

"Turnscale? That's a snake traitor?"

"Ja, ja. Gragg of Slonk, that be the old snake's name. He's a turnscale. Traded a kingdom for a quaff of bingle juice."

CHAPTER NINE

The Ancient Warrior
of the Firth

Svall swam up the narrowing lead of water that threaded like a black ribbon through the clusters of ice floes jamming the firth. The bear moved at a stately pace, nosing aside chunks of ice that blocked his path. The four owls flew overhead. Soren thought he had never seen such a graceful swimmer.

There was a kind of magic to the starry night. The sky reflected in the black water of the firth, and it almost appeared as if the bear were swimming through shoals of stars. Svall seemed like a creature of earth and sky, ice and air, water and stars. Like a weaver in the night, the immense polar bear shuttled through these elements twining them into one single and fantastic piece, a tapestry of the Northern Kingdoms.

"If this is summer," Twilight said, "I wonder what winter is like."

"I hope we won't have to stick around to find out," Digger replied.

"Sssh!" Soren said suddenly. "I'm picking up something."

"Me, too," Eglantine said. "It sounds almost like singing."

Eglantine and Soren began rotating their heads very slowly. Soren called down to Svall, "What are we hearing? It sounds like a song."

"Ahhh, very good ears you have." Svall looked up. "Me, I no hear yet. But we are getting closer. See cliffs?" Directly ahead on the land ice, silvery in the moonlight, gilded cliffs soared into the star-sparkled night. "That be where Moss roosts."

"So, what's that singing?" Soren asked. The other owls had begun to hear it as well. An eerie song spun out into the dark.

"The skog be there a-telling the tales tonight," the bear answered.

"What's a skog?" asked Soren. "What tales?"

"A teller. Skog means tell or sing. Tell stories. Tell history. Singer of songs. Every clan has a skog. The skog keeps the story of a clan, of a hollow. Listen now." He held up his huge paw in the moonlight. "Be quiet until the song is finished."

The lead of water they had been following opened up

now into a lagoon surrounded by cliffs and dotted with caves. A few rocks jutted up out of the lagoon's water. Svall motioned them silently toward one of the rocks, where the four owls alighted. When the song ended, Svall raised one paw and slapped the water's surface so hard that the stillness of the lagoon was shattered. Then two great Snowy Owls flew out of the cave's opening.

One of the Snowies was larger, presumably the female. Soren thought that must be the skog, and the smaller one must be the owl he had been charged to find, Moss.

"Gunden vhagen, Svallkin," the smaller of the Snowies said.

"Gunden vhagen, Mosskin. Mishmictah sund heelving dast," the polar bear replied.

"Aaah," said the Snowy in response. Then the two owls settled down on a rock a few feet from the one where Soren, Digger, Twilight, and Eglantine perched.

"Bisshen Hoolian, vrachtung isser," Svall rumbled. But neither Snowy seemed to be listening to the polar bear. Their fierce yellow eyes had fastened on the battle claws that Soren wore. "Ach!" the polar bear exclaimed. "Youy inker planken der criffen skar di Lyze."

"What's he saying? What's he saying?" Twilight whispered.

"Something about Ezylryb's battle claws," Digger replied.

The smaller Snowy beckoned Soren with one talon.

"I think he wants you to come closer, Soren," Eglantine offered.

"All right. Twilight, give me those sealed papers from Ezlryb."

The great Gray Owl slipped off the small leather pouch tied to his leg. Soren took it. In his head, the Barn Owl was going over his opening remarks for greeting Moss, just as he had practiced them with Ezlryb. Soren lofted and executed a small but perfect air hop to land on the rock with the two Snowies. *Well, here goes*, he thought and then he cleared his throat and delivered his speech in the best Krakish he could muster.

Soren hoped he said what he was supposed to, which was, "I am Soren, ward of Lyze. We all come from the Great Ga'Hoole Tree. I bring to you good tidings and salutations from our King and Queen, Boron and Barran. I bear sealed papers of great importance."

The two Snowies didn't move a feather but continued to stare at him. He extended a talon with the pouch. Moss extended a talon to receive it and opened it without ever taking his eyes off Soren.

"Bisshen ich von gunde goot, eh, Svall?" Moss flipped his head down toward the polar bear, who was floating lazily on his back around the rock.

After what seemed like eons Moss looked up from the papers that Soren had given him. He then folded them neatly into a small packet, all while holding Soren in his intense gaze. Soren felt as if he were enveloped in a luminous amber fog that streamed from Moss's eyes. His gizzard was quivering so hard he wondered if his whole body might start shaking. Without taking his gaze from Soren, Moss spoke in a rapid low voice to the skog. "Murischeva vorden Sorenkin y atlela heviggin Lyze y Octavia."

"Aaah, Octavia y vingen Brigid!" the skog softly exclaimed, and Moss's eyes grew misty, as if focusing on something long ago in a distant, unreachable time. The two Snowies continued to talk. Soren not only wondered what they were saying but what had been written in the sealed messages from Ezylryb. He knew that Ezylryb had written about the Pure Ones and requested recruits from his old division, the Glauxspeed, for the invasion, as well as the fearsome Frost Beaks. But there were other things contained in the message that he knew nothing about.

Moss looked directly at each one of the owls as if to take their measure, a kind of measure that had nothing to do with size.

"So you are the Chaw of Chaws," Moss said.

Soren almost gasped. Moss was speaking with just the

slightest burr of a Krakish accent. The Snowy noted the Barn Owl's surprise.

"Ja, ja, I speak a bit of Hoolian. So does Snorri." He nodded at the skog.

"Yes, we are. At least, most of the chaw . . ." Soren said with a tremble in his voice.

"And this," Moss looked toward Snorri and said something in Krakish, "this business with the Pure Ones is, I am not sure the words, a bad business — a nachtglaux, as we say here in Northern Kingdoms. It means 'against Glaux.' An offense to the Glaux from which we all come."

"Oh, definitely," Soren said. "It is even more than an offense." Soren took a deep breath. How would he say what needed to be said next? Moss and Snorri lived far away from the Pure Ones and flecks. It might be hard for them to grasp the urgency of the situation.

Soren plunged into a history of the siege and the fall of St. Aggie's to the Pure Ones. "They will consolidate their power," he went on. "They will bring in thousands of hireclaws from the territory known as Beyond the Beyond, and they will launch another attack, first against the great tree, and then against every other owl kingdom on Earth. And they will not stop at owls." Soren now looked over at Svall. "I know it is hard to believe that a creature as huge as

Svall could be affected by something as infinitesimally small as a magnetic fleck, but he could be. Imagine if animals as big as Svall became the witless instruments of one of the greatest forces of evil in the universe. Just imagine."

"So Ezylryb wants the Glauxspeed division and the Frost Beaks." Moss unfolded the paper again and regarded it. "Ja, ja, and he wants ach, hordo."

"Hordo?" Snorri repeated.

"Ja, ja." Moss nodded. "And," he said, looking up from the paper at the young owls again, "he wants that you should be trained in the art of the ice sword."

"Ice sword!" Twilight nearly jumped out of his feathers. "Great Glaux, ice swords! I can't wait. He really said that?" Twilight craned his head so he might better see the paper that Moss held.

"Ja, ja, and he said that the Great Gray would be particularly excited, he did." He paused again and looked at Twilight. "And so you are, I see. We shall go to Dark Fowl Island for the training."

"Dark Fowl! Where the rogue smith Orf lives?" Twilight said. "I thought we were only going there for battle claws. But training with ice swords!" Soren thought Twilight would burst with excitement.

It is all starting to make sense, Soren thought. *That's what the rest of the letter must have said. We are not here just to get recruits for the invasion but to learn how to fight like the owls of the Northern Kingdoms, with ice swords.*

"Yes, you are to be trained. We can go now," Moss said.

So he has agreed to train us, but we are so few, Soren thought. *What about the Frost Beaks and the Glauxspeed division? Dare I ask?*

"But it's almost dawn," Digger said. The nights were so short this far north at this time of the year that there was hardly time to fly. The sun was already glimmering on the horizon. "What about crows?"

With this, Moss, Snorri, and Svall began to laugh. When the polar bear laughed there was a great deal of sloshing in the water. Ice floes crunched against one another and waves broke over the rocks on which the owls perched. "Very few crows around here, and if they come we fly low, and — Svall, show them what you do."

A glint sparkled in the bear's dark brown eyes. And then with a mighty roar that shook icicles from the cliffs, the bear broke from the water and waved his arms and immense paws. The owls' beaks dropped open in astonishment. They were stunned by the sheer hugeness of this bear. He was at least ten feet tall. For a brief instant, his white immensity was silhouetted against the blazing orange of the rising sun. He then plopped back into the water and waves crashed, sending spume flying up several feet into the air. A crow wouldn't have a chance against those big, swatting paws.

Now the owls were really excited. It was very seldom that they flew during the daylight hours, and in this strange treeless white land with its sea of ice veined with water leads, it would be a fantastic new experience. They were all excited; that is, except Soren.

"Uh, just a minute," Soren said. His voice was tight. "I just want to know one thing, sir," he said, looking directly at Moss. "You have agreed to train us. But we are merely seven owls in all. Hardly enough to do much damage."

"You shall teach others when you return to the great tree."

Soren was getting that sinking feeling in his gizzard. "But what about the Frost Beaks and the Glauxspeed division?"

"Aah, that is a big decision. It must wait until the parliament convenes."

But there isn't time! Soren thought desperately. *There isn't time!* He watched as the owls spread their wings and lifted off. Was he the only one of the band that found this uncertainty unbearable? Soren blinked and flapped his wings once, twice, and then rose from the rock to follow the rest of the band and the two Snowies.

The four young owls, flanked by Moss and the skog named Snorri, set their course for Dark Fowl Island. Beneath them swam Svall, gliding through the water with an unmatched grace, softly batting away ice floes that intruded upon his path. The sun slid above the horizon like a thin coin gilding the water with reflected light. The bright reflection of the sun turned the dark water to a molten gold that flowed between the ice floes.

By full morning, the water sparkled a fierce blue, the same color as the sky. Everything seemed incredibly crisp and clear. It was a blue-white world and, although Soren had never thought twice about the color of his feathers, he felt almost dingy compared to the Snowy Owls and Svall, who fit in so perfectly. Not only did he feel dingy, he felt completely devastated at his failure to gain any assurances from Moss. What was to happen to all of them? The great tree, owlkind? He looked down at Svall, so powerful as he stroked through the icy sea. But for how long would this beautiful white bear be powerful, be free?

CHAPTER TEN
Gragg of Slonk

G ood light. See you in a bit, Matron. You take good care of him," the elderly Kielian snake said to Ifghar's attendant and he slipped off, just as the sun was rising. The Short-eared Owl who took care of the ailing Ifghar blinked her eyes in contempt. "The old sot," she murmured under her breath. "Off for his beloved bingle juice, he is!" She often thought how convenient it had been for Gragg to accompany Ifghar to the retreat. The Glauxian Brothers were known for brewing fine bingle juice, which they rarely imbibed themselves except for special ceremonies.

But this morning, Gragg did not slither down in the tree trunk and out to the bingle brewery in the neighboring birch tree. Instead, he began a long ascent toward the top of a tree. There was a particularly sonorous branch that was slightly vented, and which was just above the hollow of the two Hoolian owls that had arrived from the famous great tree. He wanted to hear more of their conversation. This was his chance. And he did not plan to botch it with bingle juice.

These two young owls, the Spotted one and the little Elf Owl, interested him. They came from the Great Ga'Hoole Tree, supposedly to do research. But there was something more, he just knew it. He had once had dreams of glory. But now neither the Kielian League nor the Ice Talons would have him and Ifghar. He was tired of life in the retreat. He was tired of living like an outcast between two worlds, sustained only by bingle juice, minding a dimwitted owl whom he had once thought was the most courageous owl in the entire Northern Kingdoms. He had given up everything for Ifghar. He had loved Ifghar the way only a snake who had flown atop his commander's back feathers in battle could love another species. But at this glory-forsaken retreat, Ifghar had become more and more lost in his thoughts, his gizzard, like a guttering candle, giving a flicker only now and then, his brain growing duller and duller, the light in his yellow eyes dimmer and dimmer.

And Gragg himself had given in to the juice. The old matron, the Short-eared Owl, more or less took care of them both. But she was a poor excuse for an owl herself. She hardly ever flew, except for meditation flights, because of a damaged wing. *Not the sharpest claws in the cupboard*, as the old saying went.

Battle claws! How long had it been since he had seen a gleaming pair of honest-to-goodness battle claws? He felt a tingle of joy as he wound his way up the tree to hang on a branch just above the hollow of the two young owls. *Yes*, he thought as he was approaching the branch, *I'm sober, I'm still strong despite the years of juice, and these two owls might just be our way out of here and on to glory, the glory that should have been ours.* He wondered briefly if Ifghar could still fly with him aboard. *Oh, well, I won't worry about that now*, Gragg thought and looped himself in a double-knotted twist from the branch, then pressed his head against a knothole in the tree to listen.

"Invasion? But why an invasion? Can't you talk to them?"

Invasion! A shiver ran through Gragg, causing his blue-green skin to shimmer with an eerie iridescence.

"No, you don't understand, Cleve."

Cleve, the prince from the hollow of Snarth, that lemming-livered, gizzardless . . . But Gragg broke off the thought and pressed his ear closer to the hole.

"You see . . ." It was the other Spotted Owl speaking now. Gragg could tell by the slightly baying tone she used. Sounded very hoity-toity to him. He could not understand all of the Hoolian but enough, and occasionally the Spotted Owl would speak Krakish with Cleve. He had to admit her Krakish was pretty good, as right now when she explained that one could not simply talk to these owls who called themselves the Pure Ones.

As he listened to the owls, Gragg began to realize that this invasion they spoke of really could be his chance to redeem himself and Ifghar. But, in all honesty, he knew that he was thinking of himself more than Ifghar. He, after all, was considered just a no-snake from the provincial backwater of Slonk. All the other Kielian snakes looked down on those from Slonk. Slonkish, they called them. But hadn't he proven himself when he had flown with Ifghar? Hadn't he seen action at the Tridents and all over Firthmore, not to mention the battle of the Ice Dagger? Hadn't he served well before they had turned feather and scale to fight for the League of the Ice Talons? But a snake from Slonk could get nowhere within the Kielian League. They were all so snooty. Just thinking of it made him wish that he could have a tot of bingle juice.

But no. He would not succumb to temptation. If he could make a new life for himself and Ifghar where they would be recognized for the truly distinguished creatures they were . . . *My liege. Yes I used to call him that, for Ifghar was my lord and I was his vassal. And I vowed to serve. But it all went wrong after the League of the Ice Talons lost.* Oh, he and Ifghar had tried to rally them to fight once more. But they wouldn't. Bylyric, the old Snowy commander of the Ice Talons, wanted nothing to do with them. In his defeat, he had turned against them, blaming the turnfeather owl and the turnscale snake for everything. Those last scalding words of Bylyric still made Gragg shiver. *You know what we do with turnfeathers and turnscales, don't ye? We turn them out!*

And that was exactly what they had done. But now there was a chance. And Lyze was still alive! That was the most important thing of all. Lyze, whom these owls called Ezylryb, lived. And Ifghar still nurtured his deep hatred for his brother.

So, Gragg thought, *all we need to do is find out exactly what these Guardians are planning, and then alert the Pure Ones. If they then defeat Lyze and the Guardians — because of the invaluable information that we brought to them — well, would not these Pure Ones honor us as true heroes deserved to be honored? Both glory and vengeance will be ours!*

CHAPTER ELEVEN
The Island of Dark Fowl

That's it, Twilight, that's it! Slash down on the diagonal."
Moss and Orf, the blacksmith of Dark Fowl, were
perched on a jutting needle of rock while Twilight fenced
with a member of the Glauxspeed unit. Their ice swords
were swaddled with lichens and mosses so as not to cause
injury.

All the owls of the Chaw of Chaws were back now
from their individual missions. Some of these missions
had been less successful than others. Soren was acutely
aware of this. Otulissa perhaps had the most success. In
the library, she had discovered some vital information
concerning something called cold fire. Martin and Ruby
felt that Hoke of Hock would indeed speak passionately
for their cause when the parliament convened and had
even received Hoke's assurances that he would begin the
groundwork as only these snakes could do with the other
Kielian snakes. But Soren had received no assurances and

no indication that Moss would speak passionately to the parliament.

For two days now, the young owls had been training on the island of Dark Fowl under the tutelage of Moss and Orf. Owls from two of the most elite forces, the Frost Beaks and the Glauxspeed units, had been called in to spar with them as they learned the use of ice in combat. Twilight, of course, was in ecstasy. "Just think of it, Soren," he kept saying. "The weapons we'll have! After all, we basically invented fighting with fire."

This was not quite true. The Guardians had fought with fire before, but it was the Chaw of Chaws, particularly those owls of the colliering chaw, that had advanced the art in a single battle when they had spontaneously begun to fly with burning branches. This was when they had been attacked by Kludd and the Pure Ones during the rescue of Ezylryb. "And now," Twilight continued, "we'll be able to fight with fire and ice. And they say that the ice here is sharper than the sharpest battle claws."

That was all well and good, Soren thought. But the real experts at fighting with ice were the members of the Kielian League. They had won the War of the Ice Claws years and years before. The companies and divisions of the Kielian League had continued to train all through these years of peace. Why couldn't Moss convene the parliament early to ask for the recruitments? It was so frustrating.

Soren flew off to another perch where he could see how Gylfie and Martin, the two smallest owls in the chaw, were being trained by the Frost Beaks in ice splinter work. It was a delicate and deadly piece of fighting they were learning. He sighed as he watched them. They were doing well. But without the help of the entire Frost Beaks division, he thought, they will all be flying into a gaping hagsmire of certain death in the invasion of St. Aggie's. Soren continued to watch. These splinters, although smaller, were even sharper than the swords. When they were launched and hit the right place, the result was usually instant death. But it was a challenging business fighting with ice splinters. One had to have a steady talon and dead-on accuracy, all while flying at very high speeds.

"More speed, more speed, Gylfie!" a rather grizzled-looking Flammulated Owl was shouting in her whooping voice. All Flammulated Owls spoke in low and somewhat mellow whoops. They were the smallest of all the Horned Owls, but still not as small as Gylfie. All of the small owls, of which there were few in the Northern Kingdoms, had been trained in the warfare art of the ice splinter. "Aim for eye, Gylfie, and then it goes right into the brain and then it is kerplonken!"

They had all learned the word "kerplonken," which meant "all over" — brain-dead, gizzard-dead, wings gone yeep. Gylfie and the owl she was sparring with, a Pygmy from the Frost Beaks named Grindlehof, wore protective goggles, the lenses of which had been cleverly ground from pieces of what they called issen blauen, or blue ice.

During a break, Soren flew up to Gylfie.

"So what do you think?" the Elf Owl asked breathlessly.

"What do you mean?" Soren replied.

"Do I have a chance as an ice splinter fighter if I pick up speed?" Gylfie paused and looked up for a second. A red blur was hurtling through the clear blue sky with a flashing ice scimitar. "Wow! Look at Ruby!" Ruby, a Short-eared Owl, was the most powerful flier of all of them. Now she seemed like a comet searing the sky, her feathers like red flames, the curved edge of the scimitar flashing in the sunlight.

But Soren worried. "We're going to need more than Ruby and you with scimitars and ice splinters. It doesn't matter how good you get. If Moss doesn't come through with the recruits . . ." Soren hesitated. "Well, I guess you can say it's kerplonken."

"No word from Moss yet?"

"The parliament of the Kielian League has to meet. They are the ones who decide. The worst part of it is that the parliament doesn't meet until after we leave. "

"That's tomorrow! Can't they call an emergency session?"

Soren looked at Gylfie and blinked. "Gylfie, there is one thing I have learned since being in the Northern Kingdoms — these owls are set in their ways. You can't budge them. They have their own way of doing everything, from hunting to preening, from nest building with moss and down . . ."

"To harvesting ice," Digger said as he settled onto the outcropping with Soren and Gylfie.

"Harvesting ice?" Gylfie and Soren both said at once.

"You bet," said Digger. "I was just learning from a couple of Snowies how to split off ice shards for swords, splinters, daggers, and scimitars. A very precise piece of engineering work it is. And if you think the owls are set in their ways, you should see the Kielian snakes who were teaching me how to bury the swords to preserve their sharpness and keep them from melting. You can call it 'set in their ways' but I think it is really just part of surviving in this ice-locked kingdom. There are no second chances here. You do it one way or die."

Soren looked hard at the Burrowing Owl as he spoke and when he had finished, Soren blinked. This was so like Digger. The most philosophical of all the owls, Digger was always, as his name suggested, digging beneath the surface of things, prying loose the obvious to find a deeper truth in the obscure — the hidden facets and meanings of life. Soren now flipped his head around. "See that owl, Snorri, up there on that cliff?"

"Yeah," Gylfie said. "What's she doing?"

"She's the skog," Soren replied.

"But what's she doing?"

"Skogging," said Soren. "She's the teller of stories, the keeper. I found out that skog means not only 'telling' but 'keeping.'"

"Well what in Glaux's name is she keeping or telling up there?" Gylfie asked.

"Us," Soren said quietly. "She's telling about us. What we're doing here. Why we have come. But I wish I knew the end of the story." Soren sighed.

Meanwhile, hiding in the shadows of a distant cliff on Dark Fowl Island, a raggedy old Whiskered Screech Owl perched. At his feet, a snake coiled. "You mean to say that my brother still lives?" This was at least the hundredth time in two days that Ifghar had asked this question.

"Yes." Gragg nodded with infinite patience.

"And that these owls are commanded by him, for some . . . some . . ." Ifghar tried to arrange his thoughts. It had been such a long time since he had felt that there was anything worth thinking, let alone speaking about.

"An invasion," Gragg prompted.

"An invasion of what?"

"I'm not sure. Something called the canyonlands that are being held by some force called the Pure Ones."

"I thought Lyze had stopped fighting. Hung up his claws."

"He's not doing the fighting. Those owls out there are. And they're trying to recruit owls and snakes from the Kielian League."

"Hrrruh!" Ifghar made a growling sound. "Good luck," he said acidly.

This is good! This is good! Gragg thought. *He's feeling something.* It had been years since Ifghar had experienced any emotion. It was as if in his envy and his jealousy of his brother, Lyze, he had spent every shred of feeling, of anger, of hate, of anything. He was simply resigned to being towed around by that stupid old Short-eared Owl, Twilla. Twilla had, of course, accompanied them on this flight to Dark Fowl Island, but Gragg had sent her off hunting for lemmings. She had gone without a word of protest for she was simply ecstatic that the old Whiskered Screech had, for the first time in all the years she had been taking care of him, shown any eagerness to do anything at all. But Gragg had been careful to say nothing to Twilla of Lyze or who these owls were.

He waited, then began to speak in a slow voice to Ifghar. "Now listen to me very carefully, Ifghar. Do you want the glory that was to be yours — and I don't mean Lil. I am not talking about love. I am talking about glory, power, respect." Ifghar blinked. Gragg continued, "Supposing we find out information, good information, valuable information about when these Guardians plan to invade, and suppose we go to the Pure Ones with it and because of this information they are able to defeat your brother and the Guardians? Well, do you not think that they would restore the glory that was stolen from you?" On the word "stolen," Gragg uncoiled himself and lay flat on the rock so Ifghar could better see what he wanted him to see.

Now Ifghar leaned farther out on his perch and looked toward the owls practicing fighting techniques. He cleared his eyes with the thin transparent membrane that allowed owls to swipe anything away that might interfere with their vision. "No!" he gasped.

Oh, but yes! Gragg thought. This was precisely what he wanted the Ifghar to see. The brightly polished, unmistakable battle claws of his brother, Lyze, on the talons of another owl — a Barn Owl, of all things! Gragg had first seen them two days before when he had hitched a flight on the back of a Great Gray, an old hireclaw friend of his who had turned pirate.

"No!" Ifghar said again in disbelief. "The claws! My claws. Those battle claws should be mine. He stole them!"

"Indeed, my liege."

Ifghar turned toward the snake and blinked. *My liege, he called me "my liege."* A shudder of joy passed through his gizzard. The dim yellow eyes were set a-kindle, like two small sparks that were about to burst into flame.

CHAPTER TWELVE

Stuck on a Dagger

One can think of katabatic winds as the fuel for williwaws."

"Oh, great," muttered Gylfie as Otulissa held forth on the fierce and peculiar winds that had now pinned them onto a shelf on the east side of the Ice Dagger.

"You see, the density of cold air is higher than that of warm air, thus in the wintertime . . ."

"But it's not really winter yet," Soren said. There was a twinge of regret in Soren's voice. He felt terrible. It was Soren who had pushed their departure to the last possible date, hoping that the parliament might decide to meet earlier. The dwenking had come and gone and now a thread of the moon, as fine as the thinnest filament of a downy feather, hung in the pale lavender sky. They had tried to fly out twice already but had been slammed back each time. The winds added insult to Soren's already deep injuries. He had failed so completely, it would be unimaginably hard to face Ezylryb. It was bad enough that he would be returning — if indeed they could return — with no assurances, but now with these winds he was really endangering the Chaw of Chaws. It was stupid of him to have waited. And if they did return, what would be waiting for them? There was no hope of victory without the Frost Beaks.

There was a chance that the four owls of the weather chaw — Soren, Ruby, Martin, and Otulissa — could make it out. They were experienced in flying in any kind of wind. Twilight, because of his size and strength, would have been able to fly it. But for the others it was unlikely. They did not possess the skills of sparring with such tumultuous and violent winds. But all of them were flying heavy, with their botkin bags full of ice weapons, ranging from scimitars to swords, from ice splinters to daggers.

"Believe me, that owl has more wind than any katabat or whatever in hagsmire you call it," grumbled Twilight. "Put a mouse in it, Otulissa," Twilight barked.

"If only she could," Ruby sighed. "If only we all could."

For three days now they had been virtual prisoners on this narrow shelf of the Ice Dagger. The only food that was available were the fish that were kicked up from the raging sea below them and landed on the so-called hilt of the Ice Dagger. And these owls did not care for fish any more than they had cared for sour lemmings.

"Good grief, what is that thing that just rode in on the crest of that wave? Look at it flailing its claws down there. It's been tossed on its back or something." Digger was staring straight down from the shelf, where they perched, to the hilt.

"Oh, it's a lobster — crustacean, of the animal kingdom but part of the subphylum of Arthropodea, as opposed to us, who are of the phylum Chordata, meaning that members of our phylum often have a head and tail, a digestive system with an opening at both ends ..." Otulissa began lecturing.

"Oh, whoopee! Would you kindly put a big fat phylum in your big fat beak, Otulissa! You are frinking me off!" Digger shouted.

Soren blinked. Things were deteriorating rapidly if Digger, the calmest and the most tolerant owl of them all, was reduced to shouting and cursing. Digger never cursed. Hollow fever was obviously setting in. This happened when owls had been cooped up for too long a time in their hollows. But this was not a hollow with nice fluffy down and moss. They were eight owls crammed onto this narrow shelf with their botkin bags of weapons. Icicles from above seemed to grow longer by the minute. The icicles hanging down over the shelf made it seem as if they were looking out from the inside of the fanged mouth of some major carnivore. Not pleasant. But then again, what were they to do? Icy, slopping winds were throwing up an amazing array of sea life, none of which looked particularly appealing as food.

"Now, tell me," Digger said, regaining some of his usual equanimity. "how do you eat something like that?" He was looking down on an octopus that had just been flung up.

"Where to even begin?" Eglantine sighed.

"Eight legs. Absurd," Gylfie said. "She should trade in four of them for a pair of wings."

"How do you know it's a she?" Ruby asked.

"Interesting that you should raise the question of gender in reference to an octopus," Otulissa began.

Please shut up. Oh, please shut up. I shall not resort to violence. I am the leader of this mission. I shall not resort to behavior unbecoming a leader. Soren had shut his eyes in an attempt to quell his anger and concentrate on not batting Otulissa over the head with an icicle. He felt something small nudge his foot. It was Gylfie. "Soren, what's that out there? It doesn't look good."

CHAPTER THIRTEEN

Pirates

It certainly did not. Silence fell upon the owls. Out across the water, in the spume-spun darkening night, a dozen or more owls flew toward the Ice Dagger. They were not from any of the forces of the Kielian League that they had met on Dark Fowl. There was not a Frost Beak or a Glauxspeed owl among them. But they were certainly armed, and they were most peculiar-looking. Their feathers were not black or white or gray or any of the tawny brown colors of normal owls but had been dyed bright and garish hues. Some had patches of orange and purple, others had red and yellow, still others were iridescent greens and blues. "Holy Glaux, have you ever seen an owl that color?" Martin gasped.

"What do they think they are — parrots?" Twilight muttered.

"They're kraals," Otulissa said.

"What?" Soren asked.

"Kraals," Otulissa repeated. "That's Krakish for pirates."

"Pirates!" the seven other owls gasped.

But at least Otulissa had the grace not to launch into a lecture on their phylum, genus, or species. They were, after all, owls. She had first read about pirate owls in the long narrative poem the *Yigdaldish Ga'far*, which related the heroic adventures of the Great Snowy Owl, Proudfoot, and an Eagle Owl called Hot Beak. No, it was not necessary to know what class or group these pirates belonged to. They were simply the thugs of the Northern Kingdoms. They fought for no side. They fought to kill, sometimes to capture, and always to steal. They were more dangerous than hireclaws, who fought for any side that would pay them, because basically these pirates stuck together as a band, and thus had become much more skillful in their strategies.

"This does not look good," Ruby said.

"But I'm a bad baaaad owl!" Twilight hooted at the top of his lungs and, just as the pirates were closing in, the Great Gray broke from the prison of icicles. Then, seizing the largest icicle he could manage, he launched himself on a ferocious gust of wind. Ruby followed, then Soren, but before he flew off, he turned to Gylfie, Eglantine, and Digger. "You all stay here. You're not in the weather chaw.

You won't be able to fly in this turbulence. Just keep us supplied with weapons."

"Yes, sir!" they all said. Soren knew that with his strong legs Digger would be great at prying off fresh ice shards for them, and he had been trained to do this on Dark Fowl by the snakes. *Where are those snakes now?* Soren wondered. *If only the Glauxspeed unit or the Frost Beaks would show up. If only there were a tree. If only they had fire.* But there was no time for if onlys. They had to fight. Otulissa and Martin were sparring with a glaringly bright yellow-and-purple owl. Martin darted through the winds, his ice splinter flicking in the night. Otulissa carried not one but two daggers in her talons.

It was an odd sight: a dozen-plus owls whirling around the Ice Dagger that jabbed out of the sea. The dyed owls looked like a rainbow gone berserk. They were here, there, and everywhere. However, Soren had never seen anything so small fly as fast as Martin. There was suddenly an agonizing screech and one bright blue owl plummeted into the raging waters. Twilight flew in. "Hey, Martin, gimme four!" And struck out his talons toward Martin in a joyous hoot of victory. But victory was to be short-lived.

"Watch it, Twilight, on your tail!" Soren shrieked. Twilight dove in a masterful twist through a gust of wind and escaped the tail-feather attack. He then whirled up and, dancing on the ragged edges of the cutting winds, the Great Gray began to squawk.

Gimme four, gimme five
I'll take you live.
I'm a bad bad owl
I'll make you dive.
Make you howl
For your momma and pop
Chase you around
Till you drop.
Now you goin' to hear my thunder
Next you goin' to start to wonder
He's here
He's there
He's everywhere
This big bad owl
He don't scare.

A glittering arc of ice flashed in the moonlight and Soren gasped as he saw four brightly colored wings separate from two different owls. Agonizing screeches cut through the roar of the wind and blood splattered the night.

"Ruby, Great Glaux in glaumora!" Soren heard Otulissa's stunned voice. Ruby looked equally stunned. As she flew, she stared in disbelief at her ice scimitar, with which she had so deftly de-winged two of the larger owls in a single stroke.

Suddenly, the population of pirates had decreased dramatically. The owl that Soren had been sparring with vanished.

"I think they are in retreat," Otulissa said.

Soren blinked. Yes, he could just barely make out their tail feathers as they flew back in the direction from which they had come. *What is that one carrying in its talons? It didn't look like an ice dagger. Not big enough.* Soren blinked again. Did it have a vaguely familiar shape? And just as Soren was wondering, a hoarse cry split the night.

"Gylfie! They got Gylfie!" Otulissa yelled.

Soren spread his wings ready to lift off in pursuit, but just at that moment a thick fog rolled in. It was the thickest and the quickest-moving fog Soren had ever seen. It was as if lichen or gray moss had suddenly crept over the blackness of the night. It was absolutely impenetrable. When it rolled back and the night had turned black once more, they knew that by now Gylfie was too far away for them to find in these vast frozen lands.

The stars stuttered in the sky. Soren knew if he had been flying he would have gone yeep as the horror crept through him. For the first time since he had been a tiny orphaned owlet, he was separated from his dearest friend. It was as if an irreplaceable part of him had been removed. *Might as well cut out my gizzard,* he thought. He turned his head completely backward so the others would not see him weeping.

CHAPTER FOURTEEN

The Pirates' Lair

Most peculiar, Gylfie thought. The pirate who had snatched her now released her from his talons, and Gylfie was flying, although it seemed to require very little effort. And yet escape, she soon realized, was impossible. She regarded the formation of the owls that surrounded her. The band had once done something similar to this for her when they were flying in very rough winds. They had created a still place amid them to block the heaviest winds. But this was something much more advanced. She began to realize that through this configuration of owls and the rhythmic beat of their wings, they had created a kind of vacuum that literally sucked Gylfie along, leaving no possibility for escape.

Truly an airtight prison. Clever. Very clever. Gylfie felt a very deep tremor shake her gizzard. This did not bode well. She had hoped that these owls would not be so clever; that she would have a chance to outwit them. But any owl who could invent this flying vacuum was not dumb. Well, she would just have to quietly observe them. Listen and watch. Even though they spoke a very rough kind of Krakish, Gylfie was surprised how much she understood. Her Krakish must have improved quite a bit from the time she had spent in the retreat of the Glauxian Brothers.

They had been flying now for a while, and the night had begun to fade. Gylfie took a fix on the last of the stars and the position of the rising sun and knew that they were flying in a northeasterly direction. She figured that they were somewhere between the Bitter Sea and the Bay of Fangs. Beneath them, the ice fields spread out. They had definitely left the Everwinter Sea behind them. As she looked down in the growing light of the dawn, she could tell that the cracks in the ice fields were a greenish-blue that was quite different from the bright blue of the seawater. Suddenly, Gylfie realized that they must be flying over the Hrath'ghar Glacier. The rising sun began to take on a peculiar color of green — sharp and minty — and then jagged peaks loomed up. They were an impossible color of indigo blue. *This*, Gylfie thought somewhat sourly, *must be their inspiration for color.* Perhaps when one was this far north in a snow-covered, ice-clad, completely white world, the very air and light itself became a prism and the whiteness of everything — ice and rock, peaks and land — shattered into all of the colors of the spectrum.

She wondered where the pirates roosted. Most likely in some icy crevices, for there was not a tree in sight. *I'm going to be tree sick again,* she thought morosely. But she knew that this was the least of her problems. She did wonder, however, why they wanted her. Was she a hostage? What value could she possibly have for these pirate owls, these kraals?

The pirates' lair was not in the icy cliffs of the high peaks but rather was a series of ground nests in dens between and underneath boulders. Gylfie was kept in a rock cell and guarded at all hours of the day. She was surprised to see that the land was not all glacier but a vast spongy surface covered with mosses and lichens and low shrub-like plants. She had read about land formations like this; she thought it was called tundra. Beneath the tundra, the land was frozen solid and never melted but on top there was a short growing season when berries could be harvested. At night, the wolves howled, which she found very unnerving being confined to the ground and never allowed to fly. She could, however, peer out into the main dens of the pirates' lair and what she saw intrigued her. These pirates might be clever with their windless vacuums for transporting prisoners but they were also incredibly vain. Plates of what they called in Krakish "issen vintygg," or "deep ice," had been polished to a mirrorlike finish, and the pirates spent endless hours painting their feathers and admiring their reflections in these ice mirrors. The dyes they used were made from the berries and the few sedges and grasses that grew in the summertime on the tundra.

Gylfie began to think hard about vanity and mirrors. She and the rest of the band had had some experience with mirrors, and she knew that vanity deceived, and was not a strength but a weakness. Long ago, when Gylfie, Soren, Twilight, and Digger had been on their long and arduous journey to find the Great Ga'Hoole Tree, it had been the Mirror Lakes in the region known as The Beaks that had nearly been their undoing. Transfixed by their own images reflected in the lakes' surfaces, the band had almost forgotten how to be owls. They had forgotten their purpose, their goals, and all that they had risked and nearly died for simply because they had fallen under the spell of vanity. If Mrs. Plithiver, Soren's old nest-maid snake from Tyto, had not been there and given them a blistering scolding, well, there was no telling what might have happened. Then a phrase came back to Gylfie from a book by Violet Strangetalon she had once read: *The folly of vanity is the curse of the peacock, a nearly flightless bird, happy to remain so and to strut about for the admiration of earthbound creatures. Their appalling ostentation is equaled only by their appalling stupidity.*

There was also something else from that book that was quite haunting but Gylfie could not remember it.

She peered out of her cell. The two guards were gabbing about their new tail-feather treatments and posing for each other in front of one of the ice mirrors. They were big, four times bigger than Gylfie, and they carried ice daggers, and Gylfie knew they could use them. But surely there had to be a way out of here. *Let their vanity lead me*, Gylfie thought. But how much time did she have and why, why were they keeping her? Why did they need a little Elf Owl who would be perfectly useless in these katabatic winds? She was a high-maintenance owl from their point of view. Had to be fed and guarded. What was the reason for all of this?

Gylfie didn't realize that she was about to find out in a matter of seconds. She heard a familiar sound as something came slithering down the passageway just outside her cell. Then what little light that slanted into the cave was blocked as the large head of a Kielian snake poked its snout in. Two immense fangs flashed in the dimness.

"Gragg!" Gylfie gulped.

CHAPTER FIFTEEN
Twilla Suspects

It was just after the evening meditation flight, and Twilla made her way back to the hollow, which was empty as she expected. Where had that miserable old owl and that beastly snake gone? She felt a twinge of guilt calling Ifghar "miserable." This was certainly not the way of the Glauxian Brothers' retreat. She had looked after Ifghar for years and although he did provoke pity in her she could never say she had felt any warm feelings toward him. It was the Glauxian way to always forgive, and she had forgiven him for his treachery against his brother, the noble Lyze of Kiel and the Kielian League. Lyze himself had said to her before he had left the retreat that he was sure that someday his brother, Ifghar, would come seeking mercy and help, and he hoped that she would help him as she had helped Octavia and himself when they had arrived. But Lyze had not really needed much help. He had only needed solitude and time to mend from the devastating loss of his beloved Lil.

Ifghar needed everything and yet he gave nothing. He had been cast out by the Ice Talons League. So the betrayer had felt himself betrayed, and it had driven him to dementia. His snake, Gragg, was barely tolerable but easy to ignore much of the time as he was always either tipsy or had passed out. Gragg had been the only one to stick with Ifghar. Twilla supposed she had to give him some credit for that. But in the last few weeks, things had begun to change, ever so slightly at first. Gragg was sober, for one thing. With Ifghar it had been harder to explain. She had first noticed a new luster in his perpetually dulled eyes. He had begun to fly better, and then there had been that night when Gragg had said that he and Ifghar were going out together.

"Together!"

"Yes, together," Gragg had said.

"Do you think he's up to it, Gragg? I mean, he hasn't flown with a snake onboard for years."

"He's up to it. We've already done a few short practice flights."

"You have?" She was stunned. *When had they managed that*, she wondered. "Well, a short practice flight is one thing, but this sounds like a longer flight, and I think I should accompany you."

"Twilla," the snake said firmly but in an almost kindly

voice for Gragg. "That will be entirely unnecessary. I hope you have noticed that I have not had a drop of bingle juice in some time."

"Well, yes, Gragg, I have noticed."

"I have taken the pledge."

"My goodness, I am impressed."

"Yes, so is Brother Thor. I know I can handle this flight. I . . . I . . . don't know how to say this . . ." Gragg hesitated and shook his head. "I hope you understand, but it is very important to my self-esteem and to Ifghar's that we do this flight on our own." He paused and then looked up at Twilla. "We have been through a lot, Ifghar and I. We have done things of which we are not particularly proud. But now I think we are both recovering in our body and our spirits."

Twilla was taken aback. She had never heard this Kielian snake talk in such a manner. He was certainly sober and he was modest and almost likable as well.

"Well, yes. I do understand, Gragg. I think this is most admirable."

"I knew you of all owls would understand, Twilla. You have been with us for so long."

Twilla thought back now on that conversation. It had occurred just a few weeks ago, but in that time Gragg and Ifghar had made several flights and often did not show up for meditation. She was getting suspicious. And so she decided one evening to follow them. It wasn't easy, not with her damaged wing. What's more, she was surprised to see them flying not south but due east toward the Hrath'ghar Glacier. Why in the world would they be flying toward the Hrath'ghar Glacier? There was nothing in that Glaux-forsaken place — except hireclaws and kraals!

Her wing pained her greatly but Twilla had been a great flier in her day, a great reader of winds, and she knew exactly how to work every gust, every eddy of wind to her best advantage. But now on this treeless tundra she would have to be careful. A plain-feathered owl like herself, oddly enough, was bound to stand out among the garishly painted kraals that dominated this land beyond the glacier. She was a good low flier and she could use the scant dwarf shrubs for some coverage. It was daytime, but there were no crows in this region, so any owl might be out flying now. With winter coming on there would be countless hunting parties laying in the tundra rats and the lemmings for the endless months when their world would be ice-locked. She saw one of their dye basins directly beneath her. She blinked at the swirls of pink and vermilion in the natural depression in the tundra. To think that out of this dull, colorless land they could find such colors. But she knew that many of the berries and something called tundra nuggets could be squashed and mixed with various substances to obtain the bright colors that the kraals so loved. But in fact, the kraals' colors and design work were very primitive. The Glauxian Brothers were much more advanced as painters and dyers. They, of course, did not use the dyes to stain themselves. To paint oneself was thought to be a kind of violation or sacrilege of owlness. They used the dyes to illuminate manuscripts and books.

Shortly after that she spotted a jumbled pile of boulders that looked exactly like the kind that pirate owls of the tundra would use for their ground nests. She flew lower between the dwarf shrubs looking for a very bushy one to hide behind. Then she would wait. Wait and watch for some sign of Ifghar and Gragg.

Glaux! Twilla gasped. She dived for the nearest shrub. Owls were emerging from the slot between boulders. She wilfed in a sudden fear reaction that caused her plumage to droop and flatten. The normally burly Short-eared Owl was suddenly slender so the shrub, though not bushy, at least provided a decent screen for her. And if it was possible for her to get any smaller, she did as she saw two pirates leading a very small owl out into the open with a tether bound to one leg. That small bird was the dear little Elf Owl, Gylfie, who had been at the retreat. And even more shocking, Ifghar and Gragg were following. *What in Glaux's name are they doing to this little Elf Owl?*

Twilla did not have to wait long to find out. She rotated her head so that her ear slits were turned precisely toward the owls. Short-eared Owls did not have the auditory skills of a Barn Owl, but they could still hear pretty well and, thankfully, she was downwind, so the sound traveled directly to her.

"You see, owl, this is your choice." A Snowy, who was all painted up like Glaux knows what, spoke, and Twilla observed. Probably a leader of this gang, as Snowies were known to head up pirates. "You give them the information they want," the Snowy said, "or we set you out here for the wolves. All tied up in a neat little bundle. Wolves often have a hankering for owl."

Set out the Elf Owl for wolves! Twilla blinked. The sheer brutality of it made her beak drop open in amazement.

"Not only that," another pirate continued. "If we serve you up, they'll be most grateful to us. And to thank us they will show us where the golden sedge berries grow."

Golden sedge berries — gilt. So now they want to paint themselves up in gold, and they're ready to sacrifice an owl to decorate their own feathers! This was becoming more shocking by the second. But Twilla had heard that pirate owls entertained a lot of very foolish lore and superstitious beliefs about the gilt that could be made from the golden sedge berries. The brothers at the retreat had no such illusions. They used the golden sedge berries for their illuminated manuscripts, but it was difficult to work with. These pirates would certainly make a mess of it. In fact, there had never been a pirate owl who had succeeded in finding the sedge berries and squashing them.

Then Twilla heard the thick, oozy voice of Gragg. "It's nearly morning. The wolves don't come out until nightfall. You'll have all day to think about it."

What in hagsmire is Gragg getting out of this? What is the information that horrid snake wants from this Elf Owl? Twilla was absolutely bewildered. She had to think of some way to save the dear little owl who had never raised a talon against any of them. But then a creaking voice cut through her thoughts. It was Ifghar! Ifghar was speaking! He had hardly said more than a single word or two at a time in all of Twilla's memory. And when he had spoken it was mostly incoherent, and now most shockingly he was speaking in fairly decent Hoolian, not Krakish.

"You see, little one," Ifghar began.

Oh, Great Glaux, thought Gylfie. He's actually speaking to me in Hoolian. So much for me not pretending to understand the language.

"I long for a reconciliation with my dear brother, Lyze, or Ezylryb, as I understand he is now called. It is time to let bygones be bygones. I hear of terrible things happening in the Southern Kingdoms. I hear that these owls who call themselves the Pure Ones threaten the great tree. And we all know that the great tree with its noble owls, the Guardians of Ga'Hoole, have attained the highest level of civilization in the entire bird kingdom. I, with my contacts in the League of the Ice Talons with whom I still enjoy enormous friendships and good will . . ."

Oh, bless my gizzard! What a bunch of racdrops, Twilla thought. *That horrible bird was turned out by the League of the Ice Talons. But does the Elf Owl know this?*

Ifghar continued. "Think how stupendous it would be if I could bring an entire division from the Ice Talons League to fight for my dear brother. But, of course, it would be most helpful to me to know what they might need. What do the Guardian forces consist of? When do they plan to strike against these Pure Ones? I cannot convince the Ice Talons to join us if they do not know what they would be joining. You do understand, don't you?"

Gylfie was trying to think fast. The Ice Talons had been the enemy of the Kielian League. *Would Ezylryb really welcome them? He would not settle for hireclaws, after all. Why would he take up with those owls who had once been his enemy? And his brother had been a turnfeather once. Why would it not happen again?* All these questions ran through Gylfie's mind, and at the same time her gizzard was in such a tizzy she couldn't even think straight. They claimed they wanted to know the lay of the land — the lay of the canyonlands more precisely which was now held by the Pure Ones. And then there was a lot of information they wanted to know about winds. These owls of the Northern Kingdoms had never traveled south before. They were used to katabatic winds but not accustomed to the wild Hoolspyrrs, the very deceptive and tumultuous winds of the Hoolemere sea. But then it dawned on Gylfie why under no circumstances should she give them one jot of information: Whatever they found out from her they would take directly to the Pure Ones. And that information would allow the Pure Ones to attack first, before Ga'Hoole could get any kind of invasion under way. Gylfie wondered if she would have the courage and the strength to resist them. She had heard of torture. Would she have the courage to keep her beak shut as her entrails were being torn out by wolves?

Gylfie was not the only owl trying to think fast. Twilla was desperately attempting to come up with a plan to rescue the little Elf Owl. There were seven owls who had come out from the rocky den. Two seemed to be guards for Gylfie. Then there was Ifghar — and Gragg — and five other owls, and Glaux only knew if there were more in the den. She doubted it, however, as this was a prime time for tundra owls to hunt. She blinked again. It looked as if they were preparing for flight. Several of them were spreading their wings and lofting up to a takeoff perch on top of one of the higher boulders to catch a good launching wind. But, yes, the two she had suspected of being the guards were marching the little prisoner back into the lair. Twilla crouched behind the shrub. Now was a dangerous time. Once these owls were airborne they could spot her. Odd to think that an unpainted owl in this terrain would stand out more than a painted one. *That's it! I have to paint myself. Not only do I have to paint myself, I have to gild myself in the bright gold dyes of the golden sedge berries. And I know exactly where to find them.* Twilla had once worked in the library under the direction of the master gilder.

As soon as the pirate owls departed, and the coast was clear, Twilla flew off in the opposite direction. This would not take her long. She knew exactly where the golden sedge berries grew. It was a bit tricky, for there were dozens upon dozen of kinds of sedges that grew on the tundra, but only those that grew in what the brothers called a golden triangle yielded the golden berries. For some reason, wolves had a natural instinct for where these berries grew. But most owls did not. Finding the berries did require a knowledge of geology and botany, not to mention the proper method for extracting the juice, which had to be pressed between pads of the reindeer moss ever so carefully. But Twilla would do it! She knew that Gylfie was an owl of strong gizzard and mind and she would sooner die than betray the owls of the Great Ga'Hoole Tree. Twilla would not see this brave Elf Owl set out for the wolves.

CHAPTER SIXTEEN

An Unholy Alliance

Soren and the six other young owls faced the members of the great tree's parliament to give their reports. The bad news about Gylfie had been delivered at once. The mood was quite somber in the parliament hollow, but had been lightened slightly because Otulissa had just dazzled them with her research on cold fire from the library of the Glauxian Brothers' retreat. But soon it would be Soren's turn. And he certainly had nothing good to report. No assurances that the Frost Beaks, the Glauxspeed divisions, or the Kielian snakes would be joining the invasion. The ice weapons they had brought that now lay on the hollow floor seemed to mock their entire mission. These few weapons, even if they could train owls to use them, would be enough for two dozen Guardians at most. Soren began to speak, however. He hoped his voice wasn't too shaky. His report was brief, and he was relieved when he got to the end.

"And so you see," he concluded, "we were unable to attain any assurances of support from the Northern King-doms. I had hopes that the parliament might convene early. But they would not. It was for this reason that I delayed our return as long as I could." He then added in a small voice, "It was the delay that caused the loss of Gylfie. She would not have been kidnapped if we had not delayed. I take full responsibility for that." Soren's voice broke as he said these last words.

Ezylryb had simply stared at him, and Boron and Barran had asked him very few questions. What was there to ask? Soren had never felt more miserable in his life. If someone had told him that a few minutes after leaving the parliament he would feel even worse, he would have said they were yoicks.

But he did feel worse. His talons gripped the perch in the hollow he shared with Twilight and Digger. He was staring at Gylfie's empty nest below; so tiny, no bigger than one of those teacups that Trader Mags was always trying to sell them, and so perfectly kept in that particular way that Gylfie had. Yes, she insisted that the moss must be layered just so. Soren's own nest was a haphazard affair at best; a complete mess with moss and twigs and leaves piled up any which way.

And, as if Gylfie's kidnapping were not enough, as if it were not enough that Soren had lost his best friend in the whole wide world, as if it were not bad enough that he had failed to bring back assurances that the Northern Kingdoms would support them in this coming invasion, there was something even worse than all of that. Soren trembled every time he thought of the scene when they had first returned and gone into the dining hollow for tweener. There they were — the ones responsible for snatching Gylfie and Soren when they were owlets — Skench and Spoorn, at the same table as the members of the parliament. To see those two horrendous old owls, Skench, Ablah General of St. Aggie's, and Spoorn, her first lieutenant, sharing a nest-maid snake table with Boron, Barran, Ezylryb, Bubo, and Elvanryb was enough to make an owl yarp in his milkberry soup. Even the snake at which they gathered seemed to be quivering. She was an older nest-maid snake named Simone who was known for her discretion; thus, she could be trusted to never let slip anything she overheard when the parliament dined together at her table. They did not often dine together except when distinguished visitors came. *Distinguished visitors! Those thugs of the canyonlands!* It was unthinkable. Soren had quickly left the dining hollow and returned to his perch where he contemplated how his entire world was falling apart.

He heard a stirring outside the hollow. Then the voice of Mrs. Plithiver called out, "Soren, dear, may I come in?"

"Sure. Why not?" Soren replied.

Mrs. P. slithered into the hollow and coiled up directly beneath Soren's perch and then thought better. "Might I join you on your perch, dear?"

"Sure."

Mrs. Plithiver did not say anything for a minute or two after she had looped herself around the perch and given Soren's talons a little pat with her head.

"I know how you must feel," she said.

"No, you don't. And I really don't want to talk about it, Mrs. P." All of the blind nest-maid snakes were known for their highly developed sensibilities. Mrs. Plithiver's sensibilities, however, were refined beyond even those of her species. She was like some sort of reptilian tuning fork and could pick up on every single vibration of feeling or emotion another creature had, especially Soren, since she had known him since his hatching. So now Mrs. P. let the silence settle around them, saying nothing to the somewhat rude remarks of Soren. *One, two, three, four,* she counted silently to herself. She knew it would take Soren four beats before he burst out, and so it did.

"You can never understand!" Soren was seething mad, and he did want to talk about it.

"I can never understand in the way that you can understand," she said. "But here is what I do know. You came into the dining hollow this evening and saw the very owls who were responsible for your snatching, for your imprisonment, for all the abuse and horror that followed until your escape. I understand that you are shocked beyond reason. That this is an affront beyond compare."

"And, Mrs. P., to see Ezylryb there with them!"

"You did notice that he was absolutely glaring and stone silent throughout the meal — oh, I forgot. You left early. But he was."

"So what? He was still there, wasn't he? I just don't understand it."

"Well, tough times make for strange hollowmates."

"That's the understatement of the year, maybe of the century," Soren muttered. "Look, Mrs. Plithiver," Soren said, bending his head down toward the blind snake, "this is an unholy alliance if there ever was one."

"I know, dear, but what choice do we have?"

Soren knew that Mrs. P. was right. He had heard just a few hours before that the Pure Ones had gathered new forces. They had gone into the territory called Beyond the Beyond where there were hireclaws who would join for a shiny set of battle claws, a bag of flints, or knap for their very crude spears. They would even join up for a steady meal, for game could be scarce in Beyond the Beyond.

"I tell you again, Mrs. P., it's an unholy alliance."

"Right you are." Otulissa had suddenly flown into the hollow followed by Digger and Twilight. "And guess what?"

"I don't think I want to know," Soren said in a low voice.

"Well, you're going to find out sooner or later," Otulissa said in an almost perky tone that really irritated Soren.

"Maybe, maybe . . ." Mrs. P. hissed almost desperately, "Digger should tell us."

"Digger?" Otulissa said, not disguising the surprise in her voice. "Digger isn't part of the Strix Struma Strikers."

"Well, he certainly flies with the Flame Squadron, when they are short, that is," Mrs. P. said in a voice edging toward testy.

"The Bonk Brigade is part of this?" Twilight asked.

"Part of what?" Soren was beginning to have a dreadful feeling in his gizzard.

The Flame Squadron, often called the Bonk Brigade, was essentially made up of the Chaw of Chaw members who had distinguished themselves in the fiery rescue of Ezylryb when he had been placed in a Devil's Triangle of flecks set up by the Pure Ones.

Digger lofted himself onto the perch next to Soren, then, realizing it was Gylfie's, quickly apologized. "Oh, dear, how thoughtless of me, Soren." He raised his wings as if to settle elsewhere.

"It's all right. Don't worry about it. What were you going to tell me, Digger?"

"It seems, Soren, that we have been called upon to teach Skench and Spoorn and the other St. Aggie's owls with them how to fight with fire."

Soren's beak dropped open in amazement, and he nearly fell from his perch. "You have got to be kidding. Has the whole parliament gone yoicks? It was bad enough that those St. Aggie's owls had the largest supply of flecks — even if they were so stupid they didn't realize their full power. But fire is another thing. There is nothing subtle about fire. We are putting fire in the hands of owls who are not only idiots but evil ones at that. They're maniacs!"

Soren's reaction was so strong that the owls merely looked at one another. No one knew how to respond. "I refuse to do it. I absolutely refuse to do it. Before I'd teach those monsters, I'll fly back to the Northern Kingdoms and join the Glauxian Brothers, and hunt for Gylfie. Yes, that's what I'll do. I'll become a brother and meditate and create beautiful manuscripts and ... and ... stuff. Maybe I'll even study medicine like that Spotted Owl you had a crush on, Otulissa."

"I did *not* have a crush on him. And one Cleve in this world is enough."

"Well, there is no way in hagsmire or glaumora or Glaux's green forests that I am going to teach Skench or Spoorn how to fight with fire. It would break my gizzard. And that is final!"

CHAPTER SEVENTEEN
A Deadly Glitter

Gylfie had returned to the cave stunned. Too stunned to think. Wolves, teeth, ground predators — everything a young owlet not able to fly would dread if it had fallen from a nest. Now here she was unable to fly and facing the prospect of being devoured by wolves. And what could an owl of Gylfie's diminutive proportions offer a wolf? She wasn't even a mouthful. Although she tried not to think too much about the size of a wolf's mouth, or jaws, or teeth.

Breaking through her frantic thoughts came the nearly hysterical chatter of the two guard owls. *What in Glaux's name are they carrying on about?* she wondered.

"Look! Look!" said one guard owl.

"It's coming this way. By my talons, it can't be!" said the other.

The owls' voices were filled with awe. They were almost gasping for breath. Gylfie was still tethered but she could get partway down a corridor to the opening of the lair. She peered out. The day was clear. The sky flawless. Not a cloud in sight. But what was that thing of dazzling radiance flying toward the pirates' lair?

"It's a ... it's a ..." one of the guards was stuttering.

"It's a golden owl."

"It's more than that, Vlink. It's Glaux!"

"Oh, Phlinx, we have been chosen! I just know it. We are the chosen owls. The Golden Glaux has come to visit us. You know they say that he only comes once in a century."

"What's a century?"

"I'm not sure but when he comes he will lead us to the basin of the golden sedge berries. We shall be his anointed ones."

"What's anointed?"

"I'm not sure. I think it means blessed, Phlinx. Yes, blessed, that's what me mum told me."

"But we be pirates. Pirates ain't ever blessed, are they? What's the point of being a pirate if you be so good you git yourself blessed?"

Gylfie wasn't sure which was more astounding, the conversation between Vlink and Phlinx, which, even in their weird Krakish dialect she was understanding, or the gold-feathered thing that was slowly flying toward them like a great glittering orb with wings.

As the bird began a banking turn to land, Gylfie saw the two owls crouch down with their beaks touching the tundra in a very un-owl-like posture of reverence. *Owls don't crouch. Owls don't kneel,* thought Gylfie. *What in Glaux's name is going on here?* Then it dawned on her. *They really do think this owl is Glaux!* She nearly laughed out loud. Then she blinked and looked closer. The golden owl certainly wasn't Glaux but it did look slightly familiar. Gylfie then had a sudden flash of recognition. Beneath all that gold was Ifghar's attendant, Twilla! What in the world was going on? Had the Short-eared Owl come in search of Ifghar? And why had she done this to her feathers?

Twilla looked at the two guards and blinked. She had not expected this. The Elf Owl, still tethered, had come out from the lair, and Twilla heard her mutter a few words in Hoolian. "They think you are G-L-A-U-X." Gylfie spelled out the last word.

Twilla blinked and nearly blurted out, "What?" but suppressed the impulse. *This must be one of their peculiar beliefs all caught up in the silliness about gold. Well, if they think I am some sort of god, I'd better start behaving like one. Now, what would a god say?*

Then the little Elf Owl spoke in Hoolian again. "They think you have come to anoint them but they don't know the meaning of the word 'anoint.'"

This time Twilla had to suppress a giggle. *Gods don't giggle. Shape up, you fool,* she admonished herself. She had a sudden inspiration.

"Welcome, my children," she spoke now in Krakish.

The two guards stole a look. The one called Vlink dared speak in a timid voice that was tinged with awe. "Why have you come, Golden One?"

"To anoint you. You are my chosen ones," Twilla said.

"Chosen?" said Phlinx. "Chosen for what?"

"Chosen to lead the pirates. I shall tell you where the golden sedge berries grow, and you shall go there and dip your beaks into the berries where the juices flow and come back with the stain of Glaux and be recognized as the true leaders."

Brilliant, thought Gylfie. Hadn't she heard these two owls complaining bitterly just hours before that they were always left with the dirty work, guarding a prisoner and never allowed to go out on raids?

Twilla was describing to them in some detail where these golden sedge berries grew. "Follow the dry creek bed until it turns east, and the shield rock breaks from the tundra . . ."

"But who will guard the prisoner?" asked Phlinx.

"I shall, of course," Twilla answered.

Both owls sputtered their gratitude. But Twilla interrupted them. "Now fly along. You need to be back before your subjects return!"

"Subjects? What are subjects?"

"Oh, never mind," Twilla muttered in a most un-godlike exasperation.

As the two guards lifted into the air, Twilla turned to Gylfie. "I thought we'd never get rid of them."

"You're going to get me out of here?"

"Of course."

"But aren't you . . . aren't you . . . you know, with Ifghar?"

"No! Look, we don't have time to talk. I've got to get you loose. Do you know where they keep the ice daggers buried around here?"

"No."

"I'll have a look. In the meantime, start wiggling your talon in that tether to loosen it up."

Twilla was back in a very short time with an ice dagger. But the ice dagger proved too large to work on the tether binding the skinny little leg of an Elf Owl. One false move, and she would have cut Gylfie's leg off entirely. So she left and came back with an ice splinter with which she could work far more delicately. And as she worked, she explained in Hoolian sprinkled with some Krakish words the plan for flying out. "You are not to worry about the katabats."

"But they're so fierce, and I'm so small."

"Be quiet and listen. We are going to fly into a layer of air above them."

"How?"

"We follow the steam vents."

"Steam vents?" Gylfie had never heard of such things . . . or maybe she had.

"Yes, smee holes we call them. They are scattered throughout the Northern Kingdoms. If we take the land route and don't strike out over the sea, there are many more. It's longer, but we'll avoid the katabats, and it will take you as far as the Ice Narrows. You see, the steam vents cause strong updrafts that can boost you over the crests of the katabats."

It was all coming back to Gylfie now. She had remembered Otulissa blabbing on and on about the smee holes she had read about in a book by Strix Emerilla. Oh, Glaux! If she had only listened more carefully.

"There, it's off," Twilla said. Gylfie blinked and shook her leg loose of the shreds of the tether that had bound her. But her newfound joy in freedom was short-lived. Suddenly, in one of the ice mirrors propped against the rocks, she saw streaks of color. She looked up and saw the sky smeared with lurid colors as if a rainbow had run amok.

"They're coming back!" she shouted.

"Who — the guards?"

"No! The whole frinking lot of them — the pirates! And there's way more more than before."

Gylfie blinked at the mirror reflecting them. How typical of these vain birds. They had set a mirror out so they could admire themselves as they flew in from the west. But now the sun was just beginning to creep down toward the horizon. *Suppose . . .* Gylfie thought, and the thought was as dazzling as the setting sun itself.

"Quick, Twilla, tilt that mirror up and catch the sun in it. The one next to it as well."

Twilla blinked as it dawned on her what Gylfie was thinking. *This was some smart little owl!*

"Dagmar! Watch where you're flying, idiot bird!"

"What's happening?" screeched another pirate owl. "I can't see! I can't see!"

Havoc reigned in the sky, as dazzling shards of light sliced the clear air above the tundra. Blinded by the reflected light of the sun, owls were crashing into one another. The constantly bouncing blades of light came in intense bursts, destroying the owls' orientation. Their invisible eyelids were no help against the fragments of light that exploded before them. Were they flying east or west? Up or down? The air, the very sky, suddenly seemed brittle. The tundra world of the pirate owls was being smashed to smithereens by light, light in its own peculiar way as sharp and deadly as any ice sword. The pirates were now falling out of the sky, and as they fell two others rose in flight, heading east by southeast to catch the warm drafts from the first smee hole.

And suddenly, Gylfie remembered the other quotation from the book by Violet Strangetalon that spoke so directly to the vanity of some birds. Violet had a philosophical turn of mind and she often contemplated the souls or scroomsaws of witless birds. Those words came back to Gylfie as she heard the soft thuds of the pirates falling on the tundra. *Vanity, thief of flight, source of all that is yeep, prison of the scroomsaw.*

How true it is, thought Gylfie. *How true it is!*

CHAPTER EIGHTEEN
Gizzardly Matters

He's a what?" Twilight asked.

"A gizzard resister," Digger replied quietly.

"Explain," Twilight said.

"Yes, please, do," Otulissa spoke now, her voice reeking with contempt.

Digger pressed his beak shut, closed his eyes, and tried to count to three . . . *well, better make it five*, he thought as he tried to quell his rage over Otulissa's tone. Finally, he spoke. "Soren is what Ezylryb calls a gizzard resister. It means that If something truly violates your conscience, your sense of what is right and what is wrong in matters of warfare, if it becomes too great a strain on your gizzard, then you are a gizzard resister and can choose to serve in another way."

"Never heard such a bunch of racdrops in all my life!" Otulissa spat the words out. Digger and Twilight blinked. Otulissa saying a swear word, "racdrops" — as in the droppings of a raccoon — was shocking. Otulissa might be fierce, and she had certainly grown fiercer since the death of her beloved leader, Strix Struma, but she was still as prim and proper as ever. "It's almost treasonous."

That did it for Digger. He flew up in a rage in the tight confines of the hollow and was about to pounce upon the Spotted Owl, but Twilight intervened.

"Hey! Hey! Cut it out, the both of you. Cool down Digger. And, Otulissa, take it back."

"Take what back?"

"What you said about Soren," Twilight said. "It is not true. Not one bit. Shame on you!" He shook a talon at her. The Great Gray had puffed up to twice his size. The hollow seemed so full of him that there was hardly room to breathe. "Take it back right now, or I'll smack you from here to hagsmire."

"All right," Otulissa said truculently. "I take it back. Soren's not treasonous, but he sure is strange about not wanting to teach Skench and Spoorn and the other St. Aggie's owls to fight with fire."

"Strange is fine," Twilight said. "We can live with strange. Now, Digger," Twilight said, turning to the Burrowing Owl. "Do you have anything to say about this *strange* predicament? Do you have any idea what service Soren might be thinking about instead?" Both Digger and Otulissa blinked at Twilight. This was so unlike him. He seemed to enjoy this new role of the diplomat. *Next thing he's going to be doing is asking us to share our feelings,* Digger thought. "Share" was a popular word among the rybs when they were teaching younger owls.

"No. I have no idea." Digger shook his head. "He's with Ezylryb and Boron and Barran right now. I think Bubo is there, too."

"In the parliament hollow?" Otulissa asked with a gleam in her eye.

"Yes, I suppose so," Digger replied.

"Well, then, what are we waiting for?" Otulissa said excitedly. "To the roots."

"Great idea," Twilight said.

But Digger was not so sure if this was a great idea.

Nor was Soren sure that he should be meeting with Bubo, Boron, Barran, and Ezylryb in the parliament hollow. These elder owls of the parliament perched themselves on the white branch of a birch that had been bent into a half circle. There were ordinarily twelve parliamentary members. But seeing that now there were only four, Soren surmised that what he was about to be told was top secret.

How many times had he and the band and Otulissa eavesdropped on the parliament? How many times had they sneaked down to the strange space beneath this hollow where deep within the roots the tree transmitted the sounds of any discussion that was going on above? But Soren could hardly suggest to the parliament that they should have this top secret discussion elsewhere because it could be heard in the chamber below. That would reveal him as an eavesdropper. Twilight, Digger, and the rest were already upset enough with him for being a gizzard resister. He had to think of something and think of it fast. He knew a little of what his alternative service might require. It had something to do with the passive combatant use of fire. He wasn't really sure what that meant except that he didn't have to teach thugs like Skench and Spoorn how to fight with it. Soren thought, *If this has to do with fire, why not convene in Bubo's forge where the Great Horned blacksmith owl could demonstrate? Bubo loved to do demonstrations with coal and embers.*

"Uh . . ." Soren stepped onto the speaking perch from which owls addressed the members of the parliament. "I have been told just the preliminary details about this service that I am to perform — a passive combatant fire service, I believe." The four elder owls nodded. "And I was wondering if perhaps we might have this discussion at Bubo's forge. I think I will really understand better if Bubo can demonstrate."

"Good idea!" boomed Bubo.

"But what about security?" Barran asked.

"We can go far back in the cave," Bubo said, "and if it eases your mind, I can set out a couple of nest-maids to guard the entrance."

"All right, then," Boron said. "Shall we adjourn to Bubo's forge?"

Digger, Twilight, and Otulissa pressed their ear slits to the roots but there was total silence in the parliament hollow above. They blinked at one another. "What's going on?" Otulissa beaked the words silently. Twilight and Digger shrugged. After five minutes of listening to nothing, the three owls gave up and went back to their respective hollows.

Meanwhile, Soren, along with the four elder owls, crowded into the back of the cave of Bubo's forge. Mrs. Plithiver had been called upon to guard the entrance. She was the most trustworthy of the nest-maid snakes and, unlike the others, was known never to gossip.

Bubo pushed a small blue-green ember toward Soren. At the center of the ember was a pale lick of orange. Soren had never seen an ember quite this color.

"That's not bonk," he said, staring down at the strangely glowing ember.

"Hardly," replied Bubo. "In fact, quite the opposite."

"What is it?" Soren asked.

"It's a cold coal."

"Is this what Otulissa was researching?"

"Yep. Otulissa brought back the formula for cold fire and ice flames. And from these I made cold coals."

"Can it really help us in this war?" Soren asked. He had never been quite sure what it could do. Otulissa's explanations were very complicated.

"It can indeed," said Ezylryb. "It can destroy flecks, and make Devil's Triangles ineffective."

"Devil's Triangles?" Soren echoed in a hushed voice. It had been a Devil's Triangle made from strategically placed bags of flecks that had destroyed Ezylryb's navigational instincts. It had taken him weeks to recover after the Chaw of Chaws had rescued him.

"Yes, Soren, Devil's Triangles. The Pure Ones who hold St. Aggie's have the wherewithal now to construct more than enough triangles to defend themselves against any invaders. So . . ." Ezylryb continued.

And so, thought Soren as he flew back to his hollow, *that is what my passive combatant mission is. I do not teach Skench and Spoorn to fight, but I destroy the enemy's ability to defend.* It would not be just Soren's mission alone. During the time that Otulissa, Digger, and the others would be teaching the remnant owls of St. Aggie's who had escaped with Skench and Spoorn how to fight with fire, Bubo and Soren would fly into the rimrock of the canyonlands and place the small blue-green cold coals into every fleck emplacement they could find and thus destroy the magnetic powers of the Devil's Triangles. It was a wonderous ember that Bubo had created in the fires of his forge; smokeless, barely glowing, with a deep, mysteriously penetrating form of heat, strong enough to destroy flecks at close range but not warm enough to ignite any nearby wood or leaves.

Soren almost wished this night were over and he wouldn't have to face Digger and Twilight and Otulissa. He was not to say a word about his alternative service. It would begin tomorrow and take several days, as would the training of Skench and Spoorn and their troops. Soren didn't want his friends asking questions or looking at him all funny, as they had done ever since he had told them that he was a gizzard resister. Gizzard matters were private, anyhow. There were some things that one didn't discuss, not even with one's best friend.

Soren sighed heavily and his gizzard gave a painful lurch. *Gylfie!* Would he ever see her again? Soren entered the hollow quietly. Twilight and Digger were still asleep.

Kicking a few tufts of rabbit-ear moss to the top of the heap, he settled himself into his mess of a nest and, despite his worries, soon fell sound asleep.

The rabbit-ear moss around Soren's body folded him into a wonderful softness. *I should be more particular about my nest and get more of this moss.* But then the mossy softness began to dissolve into something else. *How curious,* he thought, for he could still feel the softness but it was as if it were becoming fog. A huge fog bank began to surge around him. *Am I flying or am I sleeping?* He felt an uncomfortable twinge in his gizzard. This was just like the fog that Gylfie had disappeared into. *Maybe I can find her. I must find her. I must!* Soren continued flying through the mossy fog, looking for the tiny speck of an Elf Owl. He blinked. In the distance, he saw something glimmering faintly. It was like a dim, pulsating golden light, and he was drawn toward it. But every time he thought he was near, it grew dimmer and receded deeper into the thick fog. And sometimes he thought he heard the soft strains of a song. The song wrapped around him like a vaporous mist, but then it simply melted away. This was a very strange world he was flying through. His senses seemed turned upside down. There were things that one usually heard — like a song — that he could almost feel, and there were things that one usually felt—like the softness of the moss — that he was seeing instead, as if it were a fog. *Fog or moss? What is going on?*

Suddenly, he heard a huge clap of thunder. A flash of lightning splintered the sky. Spume from the sea, branches, small animals were hurling past him, torn up from the earth below by the violence of the storm. There was another bone-shattering crack of thunder, and then, in a white-hot bolt of lightning that fractured the night, he saw the dark silhouette of an Elf Owl frantically beating her wings. "Gylfie!" he cried out. "Gylfie!"

Someone was shaking him. "Wake up, Soren! Wake up!"

"Digger! What time is it?"

"Late. You almost slept through tweener. Cook still has some good roasted vole left, and I think there are a few slices of milkberry tart. Bubo's waiting for you, too, and says to hurry along."

"Oh, yeah, Bubo," Soren replied sleepily and then remembered that tonight was the night they were to begin their secret mission — cold coal drops into the fleck emplacements.

"Soren?" Digger said tentatively. Soren hoped that Digger wasn't going to ask him any questions about tonight's mission.

"Yeah, what is it?"

"Soren, were you dreaming about Gylfie?"

"Dreaming? I don't think so." And he didn't think he had been dreaming about her. But this was how it was with Soren. He often didn't remember a dream — until it became real.

CHAPTER NINETEEN
Deep in Enemy Territory

J ust think of it, Kludd, this dear egg will hatch during the eclipse." Nyra looked at the egg that lay in the downy nest she had made in their rock hollow in the canyonlands of St. Aggie's. "Although I still grieve for the egg your horrid sister, Eglantine, destroyed, now we shall have a chick who will hatch as the moon is eclipsing. And you know what that means?"

"Yes, yes." Kludd tried not to sound impatient. He had heard this story so many times it was becoming boring. But it was a good sign, an important sign. Nyra herself had been hatched on the night of a lunar eclipse. It was said that when an owl was hatched on the night of an eclipse, an enchantment would be cast upon that bird, a powerful charm that made for a powerful owl. Some said the charm could be good and lead to greatness of spirit, but it could also be bad and lead to a profound evil. Nyra, however, had no time for thoughts of good and evil. She only believed in power. If an owl were powerful enough, it did not matter if they were what others called "good" or "evil." These words had no meaning for her.

Kludd had more on his mind than the hatching of his first chick. That chick might not be the only thing to arrive on the night of the lunar eclipse. That night could just as easily be the one on which the invasion began. It made perfect sense for the Guardians of Ga'Hoole to launch their invasion on a night when the moon would be blotted out by the shadow of the sun moving slowly across it. It would be the perfect cover for them. That was why Kludd had insisted that they find a hollow not right within the rocky fortress of St. Aggie's, but out on its periphery.

But when would these confounded owls come? When would they launch their invasion? He had fortified the rimrock surrounding St. Aggie's as best he could with fleck emplacements. He had guards placed on the highest point of every promontory. Any foreign owl would be spotted immediately. He had promoted his two top lieutenants, Uglamore and Stryker, to the positions of division commanders and they had set up garrisons at the two main approaches to St. Aggie's: the boulder of the Great Horns, where two peaks rose into the sky like the tufts of a gigantic Great Horned Owl, and then at the point of entry called the Beak of Glaux. Patrols flew night and day guarding both areas. No crow dared approach during the day with these fiercely clawed owls commanding the skies. A hireclaw owl from Beyond the Beyond had turned out to be an excellent blacksmith. And he would make fire claws! Fire claws were special battle claws with small coals inserted in the tips. These claws were the most dangerous of all weapons, for they allowed an owl to fight at close range while simultaneously ripping and burning an opponent. They were considered "dirty weapons." Many blacksmiths refused to make them because they not only did damage to the enemy but over time they disfigured an owl's own talons.

The Pure Ones had been practicing fighting with ignited branches, as well as using the fire claws. Kludd was ready. He was ready for war. Ready for the Guardians of Ga'Hoole, and most of all he was ready for Soren, his brother. He snapped his metal beak shut, blinked his eyes behind the metal mask, and imagined his claws tearing into his brother's flesh. He could see the blood splattering the night. He could hear the breath leaking from his brother's windpipe, the gasping, ragged breaths of a dying owl, of Soren.

On a high battlement of the Beak of Glaux, Uglamore crimped his talons over a narrow lip of rock and scanned the sky. *When will they come? When?* Logic dictated that the invasion would come on a moonless night, or a night thick with cloud cover. Cloud cover was rare here, just as trees were rare. They had solved that by importing kindling for fighting with fire from Ambala and the Shadow Forest, but one cannot control the moon or command the clouds. A breeze riffled his feathers, and a shiver went though his gizzard. There was no telling with these owls, the Guardians of Ga'Hoole. Logic did not dictate to them. Nothing dictated to them, as a matter of fact. And this was eternally confounding to Uglamore. The owls of the Great Ga'Hoole Tree were completely free, free to do anything. They knew no discipline, at least not the discipline of the Pure Ones, or of St. Aggie's. They seemed to fly in loose ragtag groups, compared to the tightly drilled formations of the Pure Ones.

And yet the Guardians had won the last battle in The Beaks even though they had been completely outnumbered. What a ruse they had pulled when they had led the Pure Ones to think that they had entire divisions at the ready, divisions from the Northern Kingdoms, when in actuality they had had none! How did a bunch of undisciplined owls come up with such an idea? The Pure Ones had come so very close to beating them, and yet it was the Pure Ones who had been forced into an ignominious retreat. The Guardians' victory had nothing to do with skill or discipline, but everything to do with wits. They had won it on wits alone.

Uglamore had not stopped thinking about this ever since. All the battle strategies of the Pure Ones were planned by either the High Tyto or his mate, Her Pureness, Nyra. There was a central chain of command with them at the top, and which went down through the Barn Owl lieutenants. Beneath the Barn Owl lieutenants were the Grass and the Masked Owls, and finally down through the ranks to the very lowest rung on the ladder of pureness, the Sooty Owls. They were all Barn Owls of some sort, and they all had the word Tyto in their formal names. But some Tytos were considered more pure than others. And this, too, gave Uglamore pause. The Guardians of Ga'Hoole were just a big hodgepodge of every kind of owl in the owl universe. It was said they even had a Brown Fish Owl among them who was in charge of a unit in the Flame Squadron, and there was a Burrowing Owl who ranked quite high as well.

So what did it all mean? Uglamore wasn't quite sure. But he was beginning to question things in a way he had never before questioned, and it was almost frightening to him. And most frightening of all was thinking about what these owls of the Great Ga'Hoole Tree might think up next.

They had notions that no other owls had ever dreamed of. Uglamore nearly laughed out loud at the very thought. *Dream — racdrops! We don't dream. We don't think.* And then it suddenly burst like a great illuminating star in Uglamore's brain. Not thinking was exactly the meaning of being a member of the Pure Ones. *But it is easier this way,* Uglamore told himself. *It truly is. One can be too smart for one's own good. Can't one?*

A fine drizzle had begun to fall. Neither Uglamore nor any of the other owls at the garrisons or watch rocks noticed the two owls who had walked past them into the canyonlands. The troops of all the garrisons were, of course, looking up and out and not down.

When Soren and Bubo finally took to wing after walking, they lofted themselves into very low-level flight a few feet above the ground. Soren marveled at how Otulissa's research at the Glauxian Brothers' library had advanced the Guardians' knowledge of flecks. The discovery of cold fire and cold coals had revolutionized the way in which Devil's Triangles could be neutralized. Furthermore, armed with Otulissa's knowledge, Bubo had devised a more efficient way to detect the deadly triangles. Now Bubo and Soren carried with them what they called a true stone. Sometimes fragments of meteorites survive their passage through Earth's atmosphere and hit the ground. A "true stone" was a fragment from a particular kind of meteorite, which was rich in iron. Through experimentation, Bubo discovered that a small needle-sized sliver from one of these fragments would vibrate at a high rate when approaching a concentration of flecks and would swing to point to the source. In the past, in order to protect themselves from the brain-and-gizzard-damaging flecks, the owls had had to fly with mu metal shields. Flying with the heavy shields for long periods of time was awkward. But now even that had been improved. Bubo had forged lightweight helmets of mu metal for them to wear.

Bubo was carrying the true stone in his talons. Soren followed with the bucket of cold coals. He saw Bubo veer sharply to port and then ascend in tight spirals up the face of a cliff. Soren followed. With a prearranged signal, Bubo angled his one wing and ruddered his tail feathers. Soren flew in. There it was: an innocent-looking little pile of flecks on a narrow shelf carefully surrounded by small rocks so as not to be disturbed. Soren dropped the cold coal in. There was a brief dim glow, no smoke, and a slight sizzle. *That's that*, thought Soren, *now on to the next emplacement*, and flew off behind Bubo, who had begun descending to the lower airspace that so far had hidden them from the sentries on watch.

CHAPTER TWENTY
A Song in the Night

It had not taken Gylfie long to get the hang of flying the smee holes. Twilla had accompanied her as far as the southernmost peninsula of the Ice Talons. From that point there was a short stretch of water to fly across, but Twilla assured her that very deep under the water's surface in this region of the Everwinter Sea there was a volcano and the boiling lava in its crater created an underwater smee hole, which vented directly out of the sea, causing thermal updrafts.

"Don't worry, Gylfie. You'll do fine," Twilla said as they lighted down on the ledge of a cliff on the tip of the Ice Talons.

"B-b-but, Twilla," Gylfie stammered.

"I cannot go any farther with you. I must return to the Glauxian retreat. I must tell the brothers of this betrayal by Ifghar and Gragg. You will do fine, Gylfie. I am going to give you a song to sing. It will ease you on your flight. It is a short song but you must learn it right now by heart and by gizzard. Twilla began to sing the song in Krakish but by now Gylfie could understand the words.

> Set your wings upon the sea wind
> Set your eyes upon the steam
> Feel the billow of the updraft
> And believe in your dream
>
> Know the mercy of these waters
> Know the safety of the sky
> Hear the voices in the distance
> And believe — they will not lie.

"It's a beautiful song, Twilla. Where did you ever hear it?"

"Oh, I didn't just hear it. I composed it. I was once a skog. Do you know what a skog is?"

"Yes, we met one on Dark Fowl Island. She was a Snowy named Snorri."

"Ah, yes, Snorri. I know her well. Skog of Moss's clan, a very big, important clan. Most of the skogs are Snowies. It was unusual for a Short-eared Owl like myself to be selected. But my clan was rather small."

"So why aren't you still a skog?"

"There are no more stories to tell. No more songs to sing."

"What?" Gylfie blinked. "I . . . I don't understand."

"Except for myself, my clan was completely wiped out, massacred."

"No!" Gylfie gasped.

"Yes, massacred in the War of the Ice Claws. Ifghar led the attack. It was wanton murder. He need not have killed them all. But he did, even the owl chicks."

"But why have you served him all these years?"

"I became a Glauxian Sister and I learned that to forgive one's enemy is the highest Glauxian duty an owl can perform. And when I forgave, I truly began to heal."

"But look now what has happened. Ifghar hasn't changed."

"That's not the point. I have. I am healed. He is not."

Gylfie peered hard at this remarkable owl. The gold she had painted on her feathers had been worn away by the flight. There were just a few glinting streaks left.

"Now fly off, little Elf Owl," she said to Gylfie. "Remember the song I have given you. The words will power your flight as heartily as your primary feathers."

Gylfie stood at the very tip of the branch and spread her wings. She began to sing softly the first words of the song and, indeed, it was as if new billows of air gathered beneath her wings. She was not even aware of having flapped them, but she was soon airborne.

The song seemed to swell in her breast and propel her onward, even through these katabatic winds. It wasn't long before she saw a tendril of steam swirling up from the choppy waters. She flapped hard toward the ocean smee hole singing the song for the second time. But as she came to the end of the first verse she stopped singing. *Dream? Believe in your dream? Now what does that mean? What is my dream?*

Suddenly, all the words in the song took on a new and deeper meaning for Gylfie. When she had sung the song the first time she had felt that the song was one simply to help her get home, back to the great tree, back to the band, back to Soren. But now it seemed as if the song were challenging her in some way to do just the opposite. She felt herself rising on the thermal updraft from the smee hole. It was warm. It was comfortable. She could fly on the crown of this thermal for a long time, toward Hoolemere and home. But why was she hesitating? The words of the song seemed to dare her to break out of this thermal, to set her wings to the sea wind. *Am I being dared to dream?*

Gylfie began to feel an odd sensation in her gizzard that she had never experienced before, not a quiver of fear, but perhaps one of excitement. *But I am not one to dream. It is Soren who dreams. Soren has starsight. What Soren dreams about often happens.* There were tiny holes in the cloth of a dream that Soren could see through. But right now, Gylfie had the oddest sense that she, too, was seeing through a hole in a dream. It might even be the same hole in the same dream as Soren. *How perfectly strange,* she thought. Except it seemed to Gylfie as if they were both peering through it from opposite ends.

Soren, she whispered. *Soren, be patient. There is still something I must do.* She had to turn back. She had to get the Frost Beaks, because even though Gragg and Ifghar knew little, they knew enough to tip off the Pure Ones and that would be complete diasaster. Somehow, she had to convince the Frost Beaks, the Glauxspeed divisions, and the Kielian snakes — parliament or no parliament — to take part in the coming invasion. So the tiny Elf Owl broke loose from the downy warm comfort of the thermal and headed straight into a katabatic wind. She would fly to Dark Fowl Island, katabatic winds or not. For Soren, for the Guardians of Ga'Hoole, she would fly to hagsmire and back.

Somehow she found tunnels through the fierce winds and the ragged edges where the katabat was shredded and weak. Somehow the little owl kept going. And on the highest cliff of Dark Fowl, the skog Snorri caught sight of Gylfie and began a new song. It was a song about the rarest of flowers in the Northern Kingdoms, the Issenblomen, or the Ice Flowers.

At the edge of the avalanche
At the glacier's icy rim
Grows the flower of the snowfields
Trembling in the wintry wind.

It dares to live on edges
Where naught else would ever grow.
So fragile, so unlikely
An owl slices through this blow.

She dares the katabats
Her gizzard madly quivers,
But for her dearest of friends
She vows she shall deliver.

Like the lily of the avalanche
The glacier's icy rose
Like a flower of the wind
The bright fierceness in her glows.

The bravest are the small
The weakest are the strong
The most fearful find the courage
To battle what is wrong.

CHAPTER TWENTY-ONE
Waiting for When

W hen do you think it will be?" Digger said.

"What will be?" asked Eglantine.

"The invasion, what else!" Twilight boomed.

"I think it might be soon," Digger replied. "I think that was what the weather chaw was all about."

"Yes," said Otulissa. "I think you're right, Digger. Ezylryb seemed quite delighted when he detected that storm band approaching."

"How was Soren on the weather chaw, Otulissa?" Digger asked.

"Fine," she replied. "But the real question is, will he fight? I mean, how far does this passive combat thing go?"

Soren had been perched outside on a branch just above the sky port and heard it all. In a flash, he was in the hollow.

"I'll tell you how far it goes. It goes to the point of not teaching idiots like Skench and Spoorn to use firefighting, and that is all." He wheeled about and lighted on the perch opposite Otulissa. "I shall fight, Otulissa. Make no mistake about that. By Glaux, I shall fight with all my heart, with all my brains, with all my gizzard."

"All right!" Otulissa said in a somewhat subdued voice. "Just asking."

Ever since Soren had announced himself as a gizzard resister, Digger had sensed a separation between Soren and the rest of the band and he didn't like it. They had to be a cohesive unit. Even though they were often in separate chaws, in any battle there was always a coming together where they found mutual support and shared their strengths. Digger knew that they desperately needed to come together again in some way before the invasion. The only way he could think was perhaps not the most honorable. "Not to change the subject," Digger said, with every intention of doing just that, "but did you know that there's a parliament meeting going on as we speak?"

"To the roots!" Twilight and Otulissa both said at once.

"Yes, my thoughts exactly," Digger replied.

"Me, too?" asked Eglantine.

"Of course," Digger said.

Twilight looked at Soren as if to ask if he was coming as well. Soren blinked. "Of course!" He shook his head in dismay. Had his friends thought he had changed that much?

"And so you see, my distinguished members of the parliament" — Boron the Snowy monarch was speaking — "the enemy expects us to invade on the night of the coming eclipse, and they expect us through the entry of the Great Horns. It is the easiest approach, the way of the prevailing winds. In fact, in Bubo's and Soren's mission to cripple the Devil's Triangles, they found this very region to be the most strongly fortified of all."

Digger, Twilight, Eglantine, and Otulissa looked at Soren. So that had been his mission. Soren shrugged.

"Now," Boron continued. "Ezylryb has just returned with his weather chaw and has some news to report."

"Yes."

The owls, pressing their ear slits to the roots, heard the gruff voice with its familiar twang of a Krakish accent.

"As has been implied by our esteemed monarch, what we have in our favor if we attack now is surprise. We are two days from the eclipse. They are expecting us on the northeastern front through the Great Horns. It was the young Spotted Owl, Otulissa, who, in her preliminary invasion plan, first came up with the notion of coming in on the back side, opposite from this front." Otulissa puffed up a bit at the mention of her name. Ezylryb continued.

"We have something else that will help us considerably — a storm system is moving our way. It is forming directly out of the northeastern portion of Hoolemere. So there will be sea winds in which all of us are accustomed to flying. They will not deter us. But these winds hovering on the brink of winter shall be plump with hailstones, a fair amount of electricity, and general slop that will not please the enemy."

"But what about Skench and Spoorn and the remnant owls from St. Aggie's that have joined us, Ezylryb?" Elvan, the elderly colliering ryb, asked. "It will be a problem for them."

"We shall try and set up the kind of airtight vacuum often used in the Northern Kingdoms for transporting injured owls through the katabatic winds. I have been training some of the weather chaw in this, as well as a few other owls."

"Did Soren agree to be a part of a system to protect Skench and Spoorn and the others?" Barran, the other Snowy monarch, asked in her soft voice.

"He did indeed, madam," Ezylryb replied. "Soren is a much-misunderstood owl these days. Believe me, Soren will do whatever is required in this invasion."

"So, are we to understand" — Sylvana, the lovely tracking ryb, spoke now — "that although our attempts to enlist forces from the Northern Kingdoms in our invasion have failed, we are still planning to go ahead?"

"Absolutely," Boron and Barran answered at once. Then Barran continued. "We have the Chaw of Chaws, who have been trained in the use of ice weapons. And they, in turn, have trained others."

Sylvanaryb broke in. "But how many ice swords, ice splinters, scimitars, and daggers do we have?"

"Not enough," barked Ezylryb, "but we must go forward. It is now or never. What ice weapons we have cannot be kept sharp indefinitely in the Southern Kingdoms, and the storm system shall pass by. We cannot afford to wait."

"Are you saying we must attack soon?" Sylvanaryb asked in a very quiet voice. The owls listening at the roots could barely hear her.

"I say we attack at First Black. I believe that is two hours from now," Ezylryb replied.

"Now, Fenton," Boron said. Fenton was a Barred Owl who was the steward of the parliament. "Please call in Audrey."

"Audrey? Why Audrey?" Otulissa beaked the question, not letting a sound pass from her. But the other owls understood perfectly what she was saying. Audrey was a nest-maid snake who had worked for Otulissa's family before the Spotted Owl had been orphaned. She had come with Otulissa to the great tree and had become a member of the weaver's guild, one of the many guilds that nest-maid snakes could join. The young owls pressed their ear slits closer to the roots. All they heard from inside the parliament hollow were "oohs" and "aahs" as if the members were exclaiming over something. Which indeed they were.

"Exquisite work, Audrey," Barran was saying. "Simply exquisite." The young owls' eyes swam with confusion as they tried to figure out what this exquisite work might be.

"Thank you, ma'am. Our pleasure to serve."

"They look exactly like owls in their shape. You have really captured the form."

"Well, thank goodness we had enough feathers," Audrey said. "The molts from this past spring were quite good, and you know we store them away for extra bedding in the infirmary. Who knew we would be using them for making owlipoppen?"

Owlipoppen! The young owls were astounded. Owlipoppen were little owl dolls that parents often made from down and molted feathers for chicks to play with in the hollow. Suddenly, they realized what was being planned — a deception scheme!

"Operation Double Cross!" Boron exclaimed.

"Yes," replied Bubo. "They're already halfway across Hoolemere heading for the Great Horns. Percy, ably assisted by Nut Beam and Silver."

Nut Beam and Silver! Soren almost gasped aloud, as did Otulissa. The same thought flashed through both their minds. *Nut Beam and Silver — they're hardly more than chicks.* Otulissa and Soren had minded them on their first flight with the weather chaw. But that had been summers ago, and they had all grown older.

CHAPTER TWENTY-TWO

The Beginning of Forever and a Day

It would be an hour before First Black, but in that sliver of evening between the sun setting and the moon rising, a squadron of twelve owls had set out. These owls had been trained in special high-altitude flying and were extremely adept at negotiating winds of the high-altitude windstream, which behaved differently from the winds of the lower altitudes. In each of the owls' talons, he or she carried four fluffy owlipoppen. The owls were flying so high they would not be seen by any spotter owls from the Pure Ones, but the owlipoppen, so artfully assembled by the nest-maids in the weaver's guild, would drift softly, slowly into the lower airstreams and, indeed, be taken up by the prevailing winds and drop into the fortified region of the Great Horns. It was then hoped that more of the Pure Ones' troops would be diverted to this front.

The first owlipoppen was spotted in the canyonlands

just as the moon began to rise. An alarm was sounded. A platoon was diverted to a cliff midway between the Great Horns and the Beak of Glaux.

"They certainly are flying slow," Stryker said to his sergeant. "Let's wait a bit before we engage. Let's see how the Devil's Triangles work."

A few minutes later, a Grass Owl came back with a report. "Lieutenant Stryker, no sign of the enemy rising from the ridge of the Great Horns. Not a one. They must be very confused. Not one owl spotted since coming into the fleck zone. And the weather is deteriorating."

"Excellent! If they were coming, they would certainly decide to divert with this weather."

"I'm not so sure," Uglamore said as he flew up.

"Why's that, sir?" Stryker snapped.

"These owls know how to fly with this wind. This storm is coming directly out of Hoolemere. It's full of Hoolspyrrs and they know how to work them."

"Racdrops. They would never be so insane to attack on a night like this — full shine moon — have you ever seen it brighter? It's a wolf moon, and bad weather coming in, too."

"Sir!" A Barn Owl had just flown into the garrison.

"What's that you have in your talons, Flintgrease?"

"It's an owlipoppen!" There was a collective gasp.

Uglamore barked. "I knew they'd try something like this! I just knew it! Alert the High Tyto and Her Pureness at once."

"Nonsense!" Stryker bristled. He didn't care for Uglamore, who, he felt, was always trying to impress the High Tyto. Stryker had been offended that they had both been promoted at the same time, although as a lieutenant major he outranked Uglamore. "It's a bluff. That's all. They are trying to distract us. Don't you understand? They dropped these over the The Great Horns hoping to lure us there. But they'll enter through the Beak of Glaux. Almost as easy as the Great Horns. Mind you, that is where they will land now — the Beak of Glaux. These owlipoppen were to make us think they were coming through the Great Horns."

"How can you be sure?" Uglamore pressed.

"I just am."

"I think you should order a deployment of troops to the other side of the canyon," Uglamore said. "We don't have flecks over there. We should set up a fleck zone there immediately."

"Only the High Tyto or Her Pureness can do that," Stryker replied.

"Well, go ask them!" Uglamore shrieked now.

"They are sleeping. I shall not disturb them. It is practically the evening of the hatching of their first chick. I shall not wake them. They are reserving their strength for the real battle."

"This could be the real battle. It could be the invasion!" Uglamore shouted.

Meanwhile, on the far side of the canyon of St. Aggie's, a lone Sooty Owl flew a patrol. He was absorbed in a half-muttered, half silent conversation with himself on his bad luck of being born a Sooty Barn Owl and not a Tyto Alba Barn Owl. "It ain't fair. I mean, look at me. Am I that different from a Barn Owl? So I don't have that flashy white face. Big deal! Hey, it could be worse. I could be a Lesser Sooty. Now there's really a lowly sort of owl. They smell funny, too. If they had more Lesser Sooties in this outfit, I wouldn't be flying watch on this miserable piece of the canyon. But no. Got a frinking awful job? Bring in old Dustytuft." *Dustytuft*—he hated the name.

Once he had had a real name, none of this Dustytuft business. What had been his real name? It was something almost noble, he recalled. *Something like Phillip or Edgar. Had it been Edgar?*

So absorbed in his thoughts was Dustytuft, who had possibly been Edgar, that he failed to notice the first pile of brush. *What's that . . . ?* but he had not even completed the thought before a dreadful coldness began to creep through his gizzard. "Someone," he whispered to himself, "has been flying brush in here." Now Dustytuft began linking one thought to the next. "Those are ignition piles. Who flies the best with fire? The Guardians of Ga'Hoole!" And it was just then that he saw the first ranks of the enemy owls cresting the menacing spires of rock that scratched the sky like a thousand red needles in the night. *This is it. The invasion. It's coming. Right to me. I'm going yeep. I'm going yeep. I don't want to die. I don't care if I'm a Sooty Owl forever, if I can just live. Oh, Glaux! I don't want to die. I'm going yeep under a wolf moon. Yes, on a bright night like this, if the Guardians don't kill me, the wolves will eat me.*

CHAPTER TWENTY-THREE
The Tunnel in the Smoke

Like ribbons in the night, the lightning streaked behind the first rank of owls as the weather followed them in. The wolf moon — full, and bright enough for wolves to hunt by — was gnawed by ragged clouds. The colliers flew in that first rank, carrying the coals to ignite the fires. Soren and Martin dropped the fiery embers on the first set of brush that had been brought to the canyon in a covert operation a few nights before. Although once again the Guardians did not have the number of soldiers to compare with those of the Pure Ones, this time they had three invaluable advantages: surprise, weather, and exquisite planning. Already three covert operations had weakened or would weaken the enemy. The Devil's Triangles had been rendered powerless. The deception of the owlipoppen had distracted the garrison troops. Finally, the brush piles that would be used to ignite their combat branches had been put in place.

On the point of one of the thousands of red needles

that pricked the night, illuminated by the flashes of lightning, the commander for the invasion perched. From his vantage point, Ezylryb could observe the entire canyon. Through a series of prearranged wing-code signals, in which he would flap and fold his wings in odd motions, he would direct this battle. Smaller owls, mostly Elfs and Pygmies, had been trained to interpret these signals and fly at what they called streak speed to relay them to unit commanders. In the history of the owl universe there had never been an undertaking as difficult, as complicated as this one. But Ezylryb silently pledged, *We shall do it. We must do it.*

After the ignition of the brush piles, the first wave of the Bonk Brigade, led by Bubo, with Soren second in command, headed directly for the heart of St. Aggie's — the library where the flecks were stored. Their mission was very specific: Penetrate the library and set cold coals in each one of the niches. It was in that direction that Soren flew with Skench, his old nemesis, next to him. There had been no choice. Skench, the Great Horned Owl and former Ablah General of St. Aggie's, knew all the shortcuts into the library.

"This way," the Great Horned Owl said as she waggled her port wing.

The old fool doesn't even know port from starboard, Soren

muttered softly. How had such stupidity ever succeeded in building this evil place, he wondered. Ruby and Martin were also flying in this unit. As soon as they finished at the library, they were to fly back to a reignition brush pile as fast as they could. At this point, the Bonk Brigade would split. Bubo and the rest of the brigade would ignite their fire weapons. Soren, Ruby, and Martin, along with Twilight, would arm themselves with the few ice weapons they had brought back from the Northern Kingdoms and join the battle, which by that time would be raging. But even as it raged, the deadly supply of flecks would be growing weaker and weaker until, Glaux willing, all owls would live in a fleck-free world forever and a day. "Forever and a Day" was the code name of the invasion. Ezylryb had named it and the name seemed both hopeful and bold. *It must work*, thought Soren. *It just must.*

Meanwhile, the Sooty Owl Dustytuft had recovered himself a second before going into a yeep splat on the canyon floor. Weakly climbing out of his yeepness, he ascended and tried to focus on what he must do. He must fly as quickly as possible to the main garrison of the Great Horns and speak to Stryker. He must tell him exactly what he had seen. He was working on his speech as he flew. No one ever listened to Sooties, but they would this time. He would be precise and clear. *Here is what I am going to say*, he thought. *I was flying patrol on the eastern section of the Needles when I first spotted the piles of brush . . .*

He must have been flying faster than he thought. He saw Stryker on a ridge midway between the Beak of Glaux and the Great Horns shaking a talon at Uglamore. He forgot his speech entirely and, even before he had landed, he started screaming in the high piercing whistle of Sooties. "They're coming! They're coming! The invasion is here! They came over the Needles! The invasion is here!"

There was a sudden wind shift and Dustytuft's words seemed to slam back into his beak. But he screamed again even louder this time, and all the owls of the garrison heard him and seemed to suddenly wilt. *Finally,* he thought. *Finally, someone has listened to me.*

The library was located in one of the highest reaches of St. Aggie's, with one port opening directly into the sky. It was through this port that Soren and the rest of the owls descended and quickly overpowered the two guards who were stunned beyond belief to see their old Ablah General. Skench attacked the first one viciously. The attack was enough to make the other owl go yeep as he saw the blood from the torn wing of his fellow guard. The owl stood perfectly still with her wings drooping.

Soren blinked as he looked around. This was the very

stone chamber studded with fleck-filled niches from which he and Gylfie had escaped. Not simply escaped but flown for the first time in their lives. It was here that Grimble, who had risked everything to teach them to fly, had died defending them. Murdered by Skench. Soren could barely look at the Great Horned Owl.

They had to work fast. They were without battle claws, for if they had worn them the magnetic attraction of the flecks for the metal claws would have been too great. However, they were wearing mu metal helmets to protect their brains from the disorienting effect of the flecks. Soren was directing Ruby and Martin to the niches. Quickly, the owls dropped cold coals into each one.

"All niches filled and accounted for?" Bubo barked.

"Yes," Skench replied.

"I ain't asking you. I'm asking Soren." Bubo didn't trust the Great Horned Owl any farther than he could yarp a pellet. He wouldn't put it past the miserable owl to have some flecks tucked away in some unknown niche.

"Yes, Bubo," Soren answered. "These are all the niches."

"Good. Then let's get out of here and back to our claws. The real fight is about to begin."

With that, the five owls flapped their wings and rose directly out of the stone shaft that was the library.

How hard it had been for him, Soren recalled, that

first flight. Straight up — the most difficult kind of take-off for inexperienced fliers, which both he and Gylfie had been. But would he ever forget that first sensation once they were out of the shaft and airborne in the dark clarity of a starry night? Soren blinked now. His eyes stung. There were no stars. There was no darkness. What had happened? The air roiled with fog, but his eyes were stinging. This wasn't fog. It was smoke. The canyonlands were on fire!

An owl came tearing through the night. It was nearly the same color as the smoke. "Twilight!" Soren called. "What's happening?"

"A complete wind shift. Everything was so dry. The canyons are on fire."

But aside from their ignition piles what was there to burn? Soren wondered. There was hardly a tree in this rock landscape. But then he remembered. There were all sorts of low-growing scrubby woody plants, and they were dry as tinder. In one spot the smoke cleared, and when he looked down, Soren gasped. It was as if a molten red sea was spreading across the canyonlands. Soren was a collier and used to flying into forest fires, diving between flame columns, but how did one fly in this? The smoke was terrible. The even layer of rising heat was pushing them too far up.

"What in the world do we do with this?" Martin, who was one of the finest small-ember retrievers the colliers had, flew up on Soren's port wing.

"I have no idea. How are the low fliers going to operate?"

Ruby next flew up. There was a nearly hysterical pitch to her voice. Soren had never seen her like this. "The Pure Ones have most of the first and second assault units pressed in between the two horns of the Great Horns ridge."

"Do you mean the rest of the Bonk Brigade and the Strix Struma Strikers?" Bubo asked.

"I'm afraid so. And Ezylryb can't see a thing from his perch. The entire code system has broken down," Ruby continued.

"Can we at least get back to our weapons?" Soren asked.

"We can try," Ruby replied. "Twilight is heading that way now."

When they arrived at the weapons cache, they were greeted by the sight of Twilight flying through the smoke wielding a flaming branch in each of his battle-clawed talons and lashing out at two Barn Owls and a Screech Owl that Soren recognized as an old St. Aggie's lieutenant.

Suddenly he saw the Screech Owl stop mid-flight, wheel around, and lash out at Twilight. The Great Gray staggered in the air.

Bubo and Soren dove for the faltering Twilight, but the Screech Owl was back on them in a flash — with Skench! *What side is Skench on?* Soren's gizzard lurched. He seized the branch that was about to fall from Twilight's talons. He swung it and with a mighty whack, Skench went spinning down, down, down, her primaries in flames.

"Watch your tail feathers, Soren!" Bubo shouted. The burly blacksmith was supporting Twilight in flight now.

Then out of nowhere, flying so fast as to be nothing more than a blur in this night of smoke and flames, came Martin. A deadly ice splinter glittered in his talons. The Screech Owl blinked as if trying to figure out what was coming at him. In that split second of the Screech Owl's confusion, Martin launched the splinter. Like a missile, it whizzed through the air. The Screech Owl gasped, rolled over, and fell to earth — the ice splinter piercing its breast, a trickle of blood already staining the feathers red.

"Is Twilight all right?" Soren flew to a shelf of rock where Twilight perched next to Bubo.

"I'm fine. I'm fine," Twilight said grumpily.

"A little shaky, but he's all right," Bubo said.

"I am not shaky." And as if to prove it Twilight lifted off and headed toward the stash of ice weapons on a higher ledge. The other owls followed.

Quentin, an elderly Barred Owl who no longer fought, was the quartermaster tending the weapons at this cache. Battle claws, the branches for ignition, and all manner of ice weapons, from splinters to daggers, swords, and scimitars, were in his care.

"What'll it be, sir?" Quentin said, addressing Bubo.

"Ice weapons for these young'uns who've had the training on Dark Fowl. And I'll take my usual." Bubo's usual was a pierced metal ball full of bonk coals attached to the end of a link chain. It was called a flail, or a fizgig, and it was an extraordinarily difficult weapon to use. But Bubo was an expert. The ball became red hot when swung in a rapid circular motion and could wreak havoc in a thicket of hostile owls, scattering them like dried leaves in a crisp breeze.

"Battle claws first, before picking up your weapons, if I might recommend," Quentin said in a soft voice.

"Of course, Q."

Quentin was a very formal owl. He picked up the battle claws that Ezylryb had given to Soren. "If I may, sir, it would be a great honor."

Bubo sighed. "All right, Q. Assist Soren, but the rest of us shall claw ourselves. We must get to the front as fast as we can."

In a matter of minutes, the owls were clawed and airborne with their weapons. Smoke roiled through the night, but rain pelted through the thickness of the smoke and when a loud clap of thunder broke, the lightning appeared like a fuzzy white filament in the grayness. Soren thought that this was the oddest atmosphere he had ever flown in. But did it seem familiar to him in some way? Had there not been another time when a strange thickness in the air surrounded him? No, it had not been smoke. Fog! Suddenly, it burst upon him: It was his dream. The dream he had forgotten completely. He felt a shudder in his gizzard. In the dream it had been rabbit-ear moss that had swaddled him. And then somehow, in some bizarre way, the moss had transformed itself into fog. The flying was more difficult now. Soren wept tears from the smoke, and his lungs ached. But the dream was coming back to him and, in the distance, he saw something glimmering just as he had in the dream. A dim, golden pulsating glow. *I must fly on!* he thought. The glow intensified. His eyes watered. He coughed. But he flew on.

"Dasgadden gut vrinhkne mi issen blaue," said the little Pygmy Owl.

"I've never seen anything like this, either," Gylfie replied and squinted through her own issen blaue goggles. The twin peaks of the Great Horns lay just ahead, wrapped in a soft fuzziness almost like rabbit-ear moss. Was it smoke? She blinked. It was all coming true. The dream was coming true. Ahead in the smoke she spotted him, her dearest friend in all the world. *Soren!* Her heart, her gizzard, her mind cried out.

And, in that same moment, a sudden blast of frigid air blew a tunnel through the smoke. At the other end of this tunnel, Soren saw something astonishing. "My dream is coming true," Soren whispered to himself. "I have found her at last." As the smoke thinned in the scattered light of the moon, two dreams were about to merge.

CHAPTER TWENTY-FOUR
The Battle of Fire and Ice

I t's the Frost Beaks!" Twilight shouted.

"The Frost Beaks," Ruby echoed, "and look what's behind them! The Glauxspeed artillery flying with Kielian snakes!"

Soren would never forget the sight. Hundreds of owls, their ice weapons glistening in the night, filled the sky. Turquoise, emerald-green, and deep blue snakes coiled up into the air from their perches on the backs of the larger owls.

An unusually small Northern Saw-whet flew in beside Bubo. "Colonel Frost Blossom, sir, commander of E company of the Frost Beaks division." The tiny owl spoke in a thick Krakish accent. "What's the situation?"

"They have two of our elite units pressed into an air trench between the Horns. They're as good as trapped. Have no idea how many casualties they've sustained."

"I see you have a melee weapon with that flail there."

"Nothing beats a fizgig to break up a throng of them birds. Could use a few more," Bubo said.

"We have ice flails. I think our strategy should be to send in the flails first. Would you like to lead, sir?"

"Yes, ma'am . . . I mean, Colonel Frost Blossom."

"Just call me Bloss. Most do."

The little Northern Saw-whet banked steeply and returned to her unit to give the order.

Soren had not yet had a chance to speak to Gylfie. They had been ordered into a holding pattern, and no one was supposed to move out of formation. Except now Soren saw Twilight doing just that. The Great Gray broke away and was spiraling up toward a high ridge where dozens upon dozens of vultures were perched, waiting eerily for their next meal — the carrion of owls. Vultures were a gruesome sight. After a battle the Guardians of Ga'Hoole always removed their dead before a vulture could descend upon the body. They often kept them away with fire and when not with fire. . . . It was beginning to make sense to Soren. Who had always gone into deal with the vultures? Twilight. But why now? The battle was not over. The vultures never went down in the thick of things. For all of their loathsome ways, they were very cowardly birds. *Why now, Twilight?*

Twilight flew up to the ridge. The orders had come to Twilight by a messenger, a Pygmy Owl, direct from Ezylryb. *What a smart old bird he is*, thought Twilight. *Here he can't see the battle for the smoke, but he knew where those vultures would be.* This would be a fine piece of work, and Twilight would enjoy doing it. He gathered speed and, with an ice sword gripped in his talons, headed directly for the vultures.

The immense birds, spectral and dark, their wings hanging like black rags at their sides, looked up.

"Whatcha want?" one squawked. Twilight was flying in circles over them. He dived now and slashed at the nearest vulture's tail feathers with his ice sword. Several of the feathers drifted off into the wind.

"Ouch! Whatcha do that for?"

"No big deal," Twilight snarled. "So you'll fly a little funny on your way to eat dead soldiers. Who's next?" Twilight churred loudly. The vultures began to shake with fear. "Listen up, you idiots, you stinking scum, you lousy frinking birds. You're all going to lose your tail feathers real fast unless you do what I say."

"What's that? What's that? Anything you say, Twilight," they all began to speak at once. They had encountered Twilight before. Usually, he just squawked one of his jangling rhymes and chased them off, but now he was carrying this strange glistening thing, and he had just sliced off those tail feathers before any one of them could half blink.

"All right, I want your miserable butts over on those horns. Half of you on one horn. The other half on the other."

"Why?" asked one of the vultures.

"Because I say so," roared Twilight.

"Do we get anything for doing this — like extra dead meat?"

"You get to keep your frinking tail feathers, bozo!" And he swung the ice sword in a glittering arc. The vultures shrieked and rose in the air. Twilight followed, herding them along with his ice sword flashing in the night. Only a bird such as Twilight could find artistic inspiration in a moment like this as he drove the vultures toward the Great Horns. But inspired he was, and he could not resist.

> I've had enough of your vulture culture.
> Now hustle on, you stink butt birds,
> Hustle on and hear my words.
> You're cowards, and I'll slice you up,
> Then feed you to the wolves for sup.
> You got splat for brains,
> Your gizzards are lame
> And now you're going to play my game!

"Get on over there, you rotten bum of a bird ... Hee-yaw! Hoo-hoo!" Twilight hollered into the night, flashing his ice sword inches from the vultures' tails. The phalanx of black birds followed by the sweeping arcs of the gleaming sword made an eerie vision in the night. Whooping and hollering like an owl possessed, Twilight drove forty vultures toward the tips of the Great Horns.

Twilight caught a fleeting glimpse of one of the Pure Ones' hireclaws go yeep. Then another and another. Psychological warfare, Ezylryb had called it. Well, it seemed to be working. Hireclaws were a skittish lot in their own way. Like the pirates of the Northern Kingdoms, they held a lot of strange beliefs and superstitions. And the one thing they dreaded more than anything else were vultures on the battlefield on the night of a wolf moon.

Otulissa breathed a deep sigh of relief as she saw a gap in the air trench suddenly open. She had been fighting as hard as she could with her ice dagger, and now she saw Martin coming in with an ice splinter. Backup was here at last. "Port side, Otulissa!" Bubo bellowed. She wheeled just in time to see a Barn Owl flying toward her. It was the one they called Stryker. She recognized him from the battle in The Beaks. His battle claws were extended, and he held a burning branch. It was going to be her ice dagger against his burning branch. *They aren't any good at this*, Otulissa told herself. *They are battle claw fighters. They have just learned how to fight with fire.* She tried to remember the lessons from Dark Fowl, about fighting with an ice dagger against an enemy with a burning branch. It was scary because she must wait for the attack, luring the attacker in closer and closer, then begin a series of deceptive moves, or feints. But Stryker's branch was longer than her ice dagger. Otulissa feinted, moving quickly from one side of Stryker to the other. *A little more of this*, she thought, *and I will be able to make a contact thrust.* Otulissa began darting about, sometimes backwinging and actually pushing herself into a defensive posture. *If I can get him to think he's got me pinned against this cliff* . . . It was a terribly dangerous maneuver, because if he did actually pin Otulissa there would be no escape.

Stryker's eyes began to gleam as he saw the Spotted Owl pressing back toward the cliff. Her tail feathers were almost touching the stone of the cliff when suddenly Otulissa charged. She was under him, delivering a slice to his belly. He shrieked and came toward her, rage in his black eyes. It was a superficial wound. "Racdrops," Otulissa muttered and wondered how long she could keep fencing. With two power strokes, she shot above Stryker and then, performing an inside-out flying loop she had learned from her beloved Strix Struma, she dived, screeching,

"This one's for you, Struma!" and sliced her ice sword through the air.

"Racdrops!" She'd missed his head, but his burning branch was plummeting toward the ground. Stryker gasped when he saw what had happened to his weapon. He jetted off through the stream of small sparks that flew up from the falling branch. But Otulissa was on him, chasing him through the night, her dagger gripped in both talons. She flew as she had never flown before. Ruby joined her in the hot pursuit, winding in and out of the rock corridors of the canyonlands.

"Force him to ground," Ruby said. She raised her ice scimitar in the night, yelling, "Force him to ground!" The two owls would try to trap him between the fire below and the ice above.

Meanwhile, Soren and Martin were advancing on a hireclaw and another Pure One when Twilight suddenly appeared.

"Where've you been?" Soren gasped, without taking his eyes off the hireclaw and the Pure One they were chasing.

"You'll see. Watch this!" The Great Gray power-stroked ahead.

"Is he going to start singing one of his taunts?" Martin asked.

But Twilight was not planning on singing, as he closed in on the two owls. "Hey, stupid," he yelled at the hireclaw. "Look up there! Someone's waiting for you!"

Soren and Martin blinked as they watched the hireclaw look up and see the vultures, go yeep, then plunge into a burning patch of scrub on the canyon floor.

"Let's get the other one!"

"Gylfie!" Soren shouted. "I saw you back there."

"Yeah, no time for talk. I've brought a unit from E company. Meet Frost Blossom and Grindlehof."

Soren remembered Grindlehof, the little Pygmy with whom Gylfie had sparred on Dark Fowl Island. Now Soren, Twilight, and Martin continued the chase with Gylfie and a small unit of the Frost Beaks. The owl they were chasing, a Masked Owl, was proving tough. They would almost catch up with it and then it would somehow get ahead. The owl was an excellent flier, taking tight, steep banking turns at very high speeds.

Soren was not sure when he started to get the funny feeling in his gizzard, but there was something wrong about this chase. This owl was not simply flying away from them. She was leading them someplace. Then it seemed as if one of the canyon walls suddenly opened up in the night. In front of them was an immense cave entrance. *Of course!* Soren thought. Masked Owls are also called Cave

Owls, and they knew how to fly the cave routes that tunneled under the mountains.

But it was too late. Soren was not sure how it had happened. They were flying at terrifically high speeds but it was almost as if the cave had reached out and grabbed them. He felt he was being swallowed into a new kind of darkness.

Suddenly, an anguished voice split the blackness. "Don't come in! Don't come in!"

"Digger! It's Digger!" Soren gasped.

Gylfie felt a tremendous shiver pass through her gizzard as she spied Digger. He was standing on a ledge, his strong legs tethered with vines to a large rock.

At the same moment the Guardians caught sight of Digger, there was an awful glare in the cave, a horrific, terrible glare. There was only one thing that glared in this way. It was the metal mask of Soren's brother, Kludd, High Tyto and leader of the Pure Ones.

One thought raced through Soren's mind. *I am going to have to kill him. I am going to have to kill my own brother or else it will be the end of owlkind.* The two brothers began to advance warily upon each other, Soren with an ice sword which seemed much too long for the tight space, and Kludd with his battle claws. The battle claws glowed red-hot at their tips. They had been fired! Fire claws. Soren remembered what Bubo had said about the damage they could do to the talons of the owl who wore them. But Kludd must think it a small price to pay in order to kill his brother.

"He's got fire claws!" Digger said.

"We've all got them!" Kludd roared.

Suddenly, six more owls emerged, the tips of their claws burning a bright orange in the blackness of the cave. There was no choice. *I'm going to have to try and kill my own brother!* There was something unreal about what was happening. Time seemed to slow for Soren.

The two owls began to face off. The others, the Pure Ones, the Guardians, as well as the Frost Beaks were fighting closer to the cave mouth. But this battle, Soren realized, was his and Kludd's alone. Soren had raised his ice sword, its clear edge honed to an incredible sharpness, into attack position. The two owls flew in wide circles, delivering quick feinting thrusts meant to distract rather than cut. Soren knew what Kludd was doing. He was trying to lead him farther into the depths of the cave. Kludd knew the lay of the cave. Soren didn't. *He could lead me any-place*, Soren thought. He knew that there were dangerous pockets of poisonous gas in caves where animals often died of suffocation. *I must keep this at a standoff as long as possible. Maybe he'll get tired. I can't kill my own brother. Oh, please, Glaux! Let him just give up and fly off.* Soren knew that this was wishful thinking. Suddenly, there was a loud crash, and both Soren's and Kludd's concentration was broken. Digger was in the air! Digger with his immensely long and powerful legs had actually broken free of the rock to which he had been tethered. He was flying with the vines still attached. But he was without a weapon. *At least the odds were better,* Soren thought.

Then something sparkled like a brilliant trace in the blackness of the cave. It was Gylfie and Frost Blossom, armed with ice slivers. They were suddenly directly underneath Kludd. It was quick. Soren couldn't tell who delivered the wounding blow to Kludd's soft underbelly. But he saw his brother's blood spurt toward him and catch the bright edge of his own sword, turning it red.

Then something happened.

"Gylfie!" Soren shrieked. The smell of singed feathers swept through the cave. He saw the little Elf Owl struggling to fly with the primaries on her starboard wing, burned black and smoking. *Kludd had done this to her,* Soren thought.

I can kill my own brother! The words exploded in Soren's head. His gizzard numb, he began to swing the ice sword as he advanced. Kludd was weak. He was back-winging into a corner of the cave. He was losing altitude.

Then there was a whistling noise and a silvery blur.

"Hiiii-yah." No song. No prancing. Just a slash of glittering ice through the dark. Then the clank of metal as Kludd fell against the rock floor of the cave. A pool of blood began to form. The fire claws sizzled in the blood. Soren perched on a rock spur and looked down at his brother. He was transfixed. He could not pull his eyes away. They were riveted on the gash that ran from Kludd's neck to his tail, the bone of his severed spine jutting up through his bloodied back feathers. Soren blinked. *My brother is dead! My brother, who pushed me from the nest when I was a chick, is dead. My brother, who swore to destroy me, is dead!*

It was almost too much for Soren to grasp. His life had been shaped by the viciousness of Kludd. *Had it not been for Kludd, I would never have been separated from my parents. Had it not been for Kludd, I would have never found the Guardians of Ga'Hoole.* Soren felt neither elation nor relief. He did not know what to feel. It was all too immense, too mysterious, too confusing.

"Soren, you all right?" said Twilight softly.

Soren blinked. A silence had fallen upon the cave. "Twilight!" Soren said softly. "I didn't hear you coming."

"You mean I didn't chant him, taunt him?" Twilight said.

"Yeah."

"I killed your brother, Soren. I didn't feel he needed to go out with a song."

"But you killed him. You saved Gylfie, you saved me." Then he paused. "Twilight, do you know what this means? It means the end of the war. It means the defeat of the Pure Ones."

"Yes," Twilight answered simply, "the war is over." And surprisingly, at one moment when one of the most boastful owls in owlkind could have boasted, Twilight did not. He blinked and turned his attention to Gylfie; Digger was tending her singed wing. Twilight then lighted down by the little Elf Owl.

"Glad to see you back, Gylfie. You were great with that ice splinter."

"Well, sort of," Gylfie said weakly.

"She's going to be all right," Digger said to Twilight. "Flying will be hard for her for a while. But it looks to me that these feathers were about to molt, anyway. Where are the other Pure Ones now, anyhow?"

"They're gone," Twilight said. "The Frost Beaks chased them out."

"Gylfie . . . Gylfie . . . Gylfie . . . I can't believe it's you." Soren blinked at his dear friend.

"It's me, all right."

"I thought I'd never see you again."

"But here I am," Gylfie replied. "We are all here, Soren. We are together again — the band is together."

And the four owls who had met so long ago looked now at one another again.

"Yes, we are together again," Soren said solemnly. "And now we must go back to Ga'Hoole."

"I'm not very strong, Soren," Gylfie said. "I don't know if I can make it. And I think all the vine slings for transporting the wounded are being used."

"We don't need vine hammocks to transport you," a voice spoke up.

"Cleve!" Gylfie said. "What are you doing here? I thought you didn't believe in war."

"I don't believe in killing, but I do believe in saving lives. I went to the Glauxian Brothers to learn medicine, remember? Now, Gylfie, don't talk anymore. Save your strength. I'm going to get a Glauxspeed unit and make a flight vacuum."

"I thought only pirate owls did that," Gylfie said, remembering how the kraals had transported her from the Ice Dagger to the tundra.

"Glaux, no!" A Frost Beak had just arrived. "They're too

dumb to think up that on their own. They copied it from us. That's how we transported our wounded during the War of the Ice Claws."

And so the band and six owls from the Glauxspeed division rose in the night. The landscape below was one of charred brush and scorched rocks. Soon other Glauxspeed units fell in beside them, transporting other Guardians who had been wounded. Silver and Nut Beam had sustained injuries. And a Snowy Owl named Bruce, a member of the Flame Squadron, had been killed and was being transported in one of the vine hammocks woven by the weaver's guild for transporting dead or severely wounded owls. Bubo was one of the sling bearers as Bruce had been a good friend of his. He muttered sadly as he flew, "No, Bruce, I ain't going to let one of them frinking vultures have you."

Twilight looked down and saw the vultures tearing into the dead Pure Ones below. He suddenly dived down with his ice sword and swinging it wildly, scattered the vultures.

"Whatcha do that for?" one of the dark birds asked.

"Because I felt like it!" Twilight roared. He flew back to the band and fell in alongside the Glauxspeed owls who were transporting Gylfie in the airtight vacuum.

"So, young'un" — Ezylryb had slid into the formation next to Soren — "you fly well with those claws."

"I do?" Soren was startled. How odd, the claws felt so light now. *So light!*

"Cleve!" Otulissa exclaimed as she flew up to examine the vacuum. "What are you doing here? I thought you didn't believe in war."

"I believe in saving lives, Otulissa."

"Cleve's one of our best sky medics," a Snowy of the Glauxspeed vacuum transport announced.

"Oh, my goodness," Otulissa gasped, and Soren could have sworn he saw the shimmer of a riffle pass through her spots. Soren and Digger exchanged glances and almost churred out loud. They both had the same thought. *Was she actually flivling with this sky medic?* Otulissa glanced at them and saw how they were looking at her. She immediately stilled her spots. No more riffling. She coughed slightly and directed her attention toward the transport vacuum. "My, this is truly an amazing manipulation of pressure. The pressure differential actually does create a viable vacuum. You know, I think Strix Emerilla, the renowned weathertrix to whom I am distantly related, helped develop this flying strategy."

Soren winked at Gylfie as if to say, "Some things never change."

"Oh, Otulissa," Gylfie said weakly and paused for a long time. "It's good to see you again!"

The great tree was bustling with activity. It reminded Soren of the night the band had first arrived so many winters ago. There had been a skirmish up on the borderlands near Beyond the Beyond. The galleries of the great hollow were packed with owls awaiting orders on that night. Some wounded owls were already being brought in. The band was overwhelmed with what they had seen — metal helmets, candles, all sorts of devices, and the immense grass harp through which the nest-maids wove themselves in song.

And now, just as it had then, a gong sounded. A sudden silence descended on the great hollow. Ezylryb flew up to a large perch. The wounded who were well enough to be moved had been brought from the infirmary to hear him. The old Whiskered Screech surveyed the throng of owls. His squinty eye seemed to take them all in, every Guardian, every Frost Beak and Glauxspeed soldier, every Kielian snake draped from the balconies.

"My friends, soldiers, snakes, and owls, it was in the time of the copper-rose rain of three years past when we first engaged the Pure Ones. Many rains have come and gone since then. Winter, the time of the white rain, is about to set in. Many have died because of these tyrants. The first to die was our dear Strix Struma and last, Glaux willing, is Bruce, veteran Snowy of the Flame Squadron. This mighty enemy nearly overran us With the terrible power they held at St. Aggie's they had become a threat to all of owlkind, but we fought well; we are victorious.

"We entered this war for simple and honorable reasons: We believe in the sovereign freedom of every living thing, be it owl, snake, or bear. We believe that freedom bestows dignity and that to enslave a mind or a population denies that freedom and destroys that dignity. If our civilization is to endure, and flourish, it will only do so in freedom and dignity.

"Now is the moment when we must give our heartfelt thanks and tribute to our brothers and sisters from the Northern Kingdoms without whose immense support our task would have been doomed. Frost Beaks! Glauxspeed division! Ice Daggers! Kielian snakes! We thank you and salute your courage."

At this, a mighty hooting broke out from the owls of Ga'Hoole as they cheered the warriors from the Northern Kingdoms. After several minutes, Ezylryb pumped his wings as a sign for quiet. "Great sacrifices have been made these past years. I wish I could look into the future and assure you that there will be no more. But one can never be certain. We have seen how the Pure Ones distorted the single word 'pure' until it became synonymous with hatred, destruction, and despotism; how they created a society in which one breed of owl was pitted against another. We must remain vigilant so that this evil does not rise again.

"Our ideals are simple: honor and freedom. We must be sure that these words are never distorted from their true meaning. To do this shall require constant watchfulness. The war is over but we must not rest. I would be remiss if I still did not cry out: Whenever tyranny threatens, fly forward; unflinching, unswerving, indomitable, until peace is restored and all the kingdoms of owlkind are safe."

CHAPTER TWENTY-FIVE

Scrooms in the Night

Deep in the canyonlands where the vultures still stalked the dead, in a hollow in the cleft of a scorched rocky cliff, a mother owl wept as her first chick hatched out of its shell just as the moon began to reappear. "You came at the time of the eclipse, little one. So I shall call you the name of all male chicks hatched at such a time. Nyroc is your name, my hatchling. You shall grow up to be strong and fierce like your father." The little chick opened one puffy eye and blinked at the beautiful moon-face of his mum.

Far across the sea of Hoolemere, on the Island of Hoole, the same moon shone. It was the last night of the copper-rose rain, just before the time of the white rain, when the Ga'Hoole berry vines turn white. Gylfie and Soren had decided to fly to a very high perch on the far side of the Island of Hoole. For tonight was the night of the lunar eclipse, and it was said that the lunar eclipse that fell on the the last night of autumn was always the most beautiful eclipse of all.

Just as the shadow of the earth began to steal over the edge of the moon, the two old friends arrived at the perch high in a fir tree. It was the only fir tree on the Island of Hoole and similar to the one Soren had lived in so briefly with his mum and da. It had been Gylfie's idea to come to this tree to watch the eclipse away from the other owls. She knew that in his very private way, Soren was still deeply disturbed by his brother's death. Over and over they had told him that there had been no choice, that Kludd had to be destroyed. But Gylfie realized that no amount of assurance from Digger, Twilight, and herself could ease his mind. She could tell that Soren was still suffering in some way. He had been incredibly quiet. Gylfie knew that Mrs. Plithiver had come to the hollow several times and tried to talk to Soren but he had been unresponsive. Finally, Gylfie had decided that it might help Soren to be away from the great tree on this particular night.

More than once he had said to Gylfie, and only to Gylfie, "I think Mum and Da would understand about Kludd. Don't you, Gylf?" And she would always answer, "Yes." He was asking her again when they heard a rustle from behind, and Eglantine lighted down on the branch next to them.

"Eglantine, what are you doing here?" Soren asked, somewhat surprised.

"Same thing you are. Here to see the eclipse."

Soren felt a little bad that he had not invited his sister to come along. But he had been so distracted in the two days since his return.

"Oh, look," Eglantine said, "it's taking its first bite out of the moon."

Slowly and silently, they watched the earth's shadow steal across the moon. It was especially splendid. The moon shimmered gold. It was as if some of the sun's gold had been borrowed briefly to make the moon glow even more before it became completely dark. Then, just as the moon vanished, Soren noticed something wispy in the night. Perhaps it was some mist swirling up from the ground fog below.

"Is it snowing?" Eglantine asked.

Soren turned to her and blinked. "I don't think so. Why do you ask?"

Eglantine blinked rapidly several times and, leaning out from her perch, peered into the night. "I see something," she said.

"I don't see anything," Gylfie said. "Look up, you two. The shadow is sliding away. You can just begin to see the moon's edge again."

But Soren and Eglantine were not looking up. They were looking straight out at what Eglantine had first thought was snow, and Soren thought was fog. It was pulling together into a vaguely familiar mass. It looked soft and puffy like the best down that a mum picks from her breast for a newly hatched chick.

I'm not going to be scared, thought Eglantine, and she felt a strange calm spread through her.

Of course you're not, dear.

How had that happened? Eglantine wondered. *I heard a voice but there was no sound.*

They've come, Eglantine. It was Soren's voice, but she heard the words he spoke in her head, not out loud. She swiveled her head to look at him.

He looked at her. Then she knew. Their parents' scrooms had come back to them. Two pale misty shapes, two dear shapes flew overhead.

We've come back, dearest children.

Not for good? Eglantine heard her own voice speak tentatively in her head.

Then it was Soren's voice she heard. *Is it the unfinished business that you first told me about in the Spirit Woods?*

Yes. And now it is finished, Soren. Glaux bless, it is finished. It was his mum speaking now.

There was no place for Kludd in the kingdom of owls, his da said.

Nor on Earth, their mum added.

The moon was coming back, little by little. Gylfie looked at Soren and Eglantine. The night was perfectly clear to her. But she knew that something was happening to her best friend and his sister. She had had a feeling about coming here on this night, to this particular tree. She never could have explained it to anyone, but she just had a feeling that in some way this might help Soren.

The scrooms had begun to fade. But Soren and Eglantine were not sad. They knew that somewhere in glaumora their mum and da could now rest. Soren knew now that what had happened to his brother had to happen, and his parents understood. And that was all he really needed to know.

OWLS
and others
from

GUARDIANS *of* GA'HOOLE
The Burning

The Band

SOREN: Barn Owl, *Tyto alba*, from the Forest Kingdom of Tyto; a Guardian at the Great Ga'Hoole Tree

GYLFIE: Elf Owl, *Micranthene whitneyi*, from the Desert Kingdom of Kuneer; Soren's best friend; a Guardian at the Great Ga'Hoole Tree

TWILIGHT: Great Gray Owl, *Strix nebulosa*, free flier, orphaned within hours of hatching; a Guardian at the Great Ga'Hoole Tree

DIGGER: Burrowing Owl, *Speotyto cunicularius*, from the Desert Kingdom of Kuneer; lost in the desert after attack in which his brother was killed by owls from St. Aegolius; a Guardian at the Great Ga'Hoole Tree

The Leaders of the Great Ga'Hoole Tree

BORON: Snowy Owl, *Nyctea scandiaca*, the King of Hoole

BARRAN: Snowy Owl, *Nyctea scandiaca*, the Queen of Hoole

EZYLRYB: Whiskered Screech Owl, *Otus trichopsis*, the wise weather and colliering ryb at the Great Ga'Hoole Tree; Soren's mentor (also known as LYZE OF KIEL)

STRIX STRUMA: Spotted Owl, *Strix occidentalis*, the dignified navigation ryb at the Great Ga'Hoole Tree; killed in the battle against the Pure Ones

DEWLAP: Burrowing Owl, *Speotyto cunicularius*, former Ga'Hoolology ryb at the Great Ga'Hoole Tree; traitor during the siege of the Great Ga'Hoole Tree

SYLVANA: Burrowing Owl, *Speotyto cunicularius*, a young ryb at the Great Ga'Hoole Tree

Others at the Great Ga'Hoole Tree

OTULISSA: Spotted Owl, *Strix occidentalis*, a Guardian of prestigious lineage at the Great Ga'Hoole Tree

MARTIN: Northern Saw-whet Owl, *Aegolius acadicus*, in Ezylryb's chaw with Soren

RUBY: Short-eared Owl, *Asio flammeus*, in Ezylryb's chaw with Soren

EGLANTINE: Barn Owl, *Tyto alba*, Soren's younger sister

MADAME PLONK: Snowy Owl, *Nyctea scandiaca*, the elegant singer of the Great Ga'Hoole Tree

BUBO: Great Horned Owl, *Bubo virginianus*, the blacksmith of the Great Ga'Hoole Tree

MRS. PLITHIVER: blind snake, formerly the nest-maid for Soren's family; now a member of the harp guild at the Great Ga'Hoole Tree

OCTAVIA: Kielian snake, nest-maid for Madame Plonk and Ezylryb (also known as BRIGID)

The Pure Ones
KLUDD: Barn Owl, *Tyto alba*, Soren and Eglantine's older brother; leader of the Pure Ones (also known as METAL BEAK and HIGH TYTO)

NYRA: Barn Owl, *Tyto alba*, Kludd's mate

WORTMORE: Barn Owl, *Tyto alba*, a Pure Guard lieutenant

UGLAMORE: Barn Owl, *Tyto alba*, a Pure Guard lieutenant

STRYKER: Barn Owl, *Tyto alba*, a Pure One lieutenant major under Nyra

Leaders of St. Aegolius Academy for Orphaned Owls
SKENCH: Great Horned Owl, *Bubo virginianus*, the Ablah General of St. Aegolius Academy for Orphaned Owls

It's the hatchling," a young owl said as the group watched Nyroc, only son of the great warrior Kludd, begin a power dive. He grasped a charred branch from the ground in his beak and in one swift movement rose seamlessly again into the air brandishing it before him. He had performed the retrieval perfectly and was swinging the branch with great style. And this was just his first flight. A power dive on a first flight was an outrageous and daring maneuver to attempt and he had executed it flawlessly. He then carved a perfect figure eight in the sky above the two large peaks known as the Great Horns. This was followed by spiraling descent to a slide-in landing on the ledge where his elders perched. His angle of approach was superb. Then, in front of his mother and her top lieutenants, the hatchling raised his starboard wing and shreed, "Hail, Kludd! Supreme Commander of the Tytonic Union of Pure Ones! Hail, Her Pureness General Mam, Nyra, beloved mate of the late High Tyto Kludd!"

Out past the reach of the Ga'Hoole Tree, where survival is the only law, live the Wolves of the Beyond.

New from Kathryn Lasky

WOLVES OF THE BEYOND

In the harsh wilderness beyond Ga'Hoole, a wolf mother hides in fear. Her newborn pup has a twisted paw. The mother knows the rigid rules of her kind. The pack cannot have weakness. Her pup must be abandoned—condemned to die. But the pup, Faolan, does the unthinkable. He survives. This is his story—the story of a wolf pup who rises up to change forever the Wolves of the Beyond.

■SCHOLASTIC
www.scholastic.com

WOLVES

Kathryn Lasky has had a long fascination with owls. Several years ago, she began doing extensive research about these birds and their behaviors. She thought that she would someday write a nonfiction book about owls illustrated with photographs by her husband, Christopher Knight. She realized, though, that this would indeed be difficult since owls are shy, nocturnal creatures. So she decided to write a fantasy about a world of owls. Even though it is an imaginary world in which owls can speak, think, and dream, she wanted to include as much of their natural history as she could.

Kathryn Lasky has written many books, both fiction and nonfiction, including *Sugaring Time*, for which she won a Newbery Honor. Among her fiction books are *The Night Journey*, a winner of the National Jewish Book Award, and *Beyond the Burning Time*, an ALA Best Book for Young Adults, as well as the Daughters of the Sea and Wolves of the Beyond series. She has also received the Boston Globe-Horn Book Award and the Washington Post Children's Book Guild Award for her contribution to nonfiction.

Lasky and her husband live in Cambridge, Massachusetts.